Walt Disney's

MICKEY MOUSE

kaboom!

For information regarding the CPSIA on this printed material, call: (203) 595-3636 and provide reference #EAST – 71475. A catalog record of this book is available from OCLC and from the BOOM! Studios website, www.boom-studios.com, on the Librarians Page.

KABOOM!, 6310 San Vicente Boulevard, Suite 107, Los Angeles, CA 90048-5457. Printed in USA. First Printing. ISBN: 978-1-60886-630-4

AND THE ORBITING NIGHTMARE

MICKEY MOUSE AND THE ORBITING NIGHTMARE

STORY AND PENCILS
CASTY

INKS
MICHELE MAZZON

TRANSLATION
STEFANIA BRONZONI

LETTERS
DERON BENNETT

MICKEY MOUSE AND THE MENACE FROM THE FUTURE

STORY AND ART
CASTY

TRANSLATION
DAVID GERSTEIN

LETTERS
DERON BENNETT

TOMB OF GOOFULA

STORY
MARV WOLFMAN
PENCILS
GENE COLAN
INKS
TOM PALMER

TIDY FRIDAY

ART
JACK BRADBURY
COLORS
DIEGO JOURDAN

A GOOFY LOOK AT ROMANCE

STORY
MARCELO MILANI
ART
ALUIR AMÂNCIO
TRANSLATION
SAIDA TEMOFONTE
LETTERS
DERON BENNETT

PLUTO AT THE BEACH

STORY
DON CHRISTENSEN
ART
JACK BRADBURY
COLORS
RACHELLE ROSENBERG

COVER
CASTY

DESIGNER
STEPHANIE GONZAGA
EDITOR
CHRISTOPHER MEYER

SPECIAL THANKS:
JESSE POST, STEVE BEHLING, ROB TOKAR AND BRYCE VANKOOTEN

MICKEY MOUSE
AND THE ORBITING NIGHTMARE

AM I LATE? DID I MISS IT?
HURRY, MINNIE! IT'S JUST ABOUT TO START!
TARADA-TARADAAA...
MBC NEWS
MBC

...ONE GIANT LEAP FOR MANKIND...WHO LOVE VACATIONS! TOMORROW, STARBUCK ENTERPRISES WILL LAUNCH A SPACE SHUTTLE WITH THE FIRST SPACE TOURISTS!
STARBUCK enterprises
MBC

THEY'RE LEAVING FOR A WEEK OF "SPACE-CATION" ABOARD THE BRAND-NEW, FUTURISTIC ORBITING PALACE: THE OLYMPUS HOTEL!
MBC

LET'S HOPE THEY'RE CAREFUL! RUMOR HAS IT THAT, DURING CONSTRUCTION OF THE PALACE, SOME OF THE WORKERS MYSTERIOUSLY DISAPPEARED!
ER...WELL...

IS THAT TRUE, MR. STARBUCK?
REPORTS HAVE BEEN EXAGGERATED, I'M SURE! SOME OF OUR WORKERS ARE JUST ON, UH, TEMPORARY HOLIDAY!
INDEED!

THERE'S NO RELATION TO ANY SPACE PHENOMENA, WHICH ARE MERELY RUMORS ANYHOW!
THE REASSURING WORDS OF ALISTAIR ZOND, GENIUS DESIGNER OF THE OLYMPUS!

THE SPACE-VACATION WILL BE A SUCCESS WITHOUT EQUAL! SCORES OF CELEBRITIES AND VIPS ARE HERE TO TAKE PART IN OUR HISTORIC FIRST HOLIDAY AMONG THE STARS!
OOH! CELEBRITIES!
LET'S MEET THEM!

HERE WE HAVE HEISMOUSE TROPHY WINNER TRIP HOVER!
WHAT MUSCLE!

AND ACTRESS BELLA BREAKHEARTS, STAR OF EVERY VAMPIRE MOVIE THIS YEAR!
WHAT A HOT--
GRUNT!
--EVENING THIS IS! I NEED A DRINK!

HERE'S CASSANDRA DOT, JOURNALIST AND WRITER OF SEVERAL SCIENTIFIC EXPOSÉS BOTH HEAVILY RESEARCHED AND COMPLETELY UNRELIABLE!
BLINK
I'M NOT UNRELIABLE!
Cassandra Dot - Monsters on Mars: the Proof!
Cassandra Dot
Monster Atlantis
C. DOT
WATCH OUT!

ACCORDING TO YOU, MONSTERS ARE EVERYWHERE...EVEN UNDER MY BED!
MY BOOKS SELL, SO THE PUBLIC MUST BE HAPPY-- AND SO IS MY PUBLISHER! IT'S NOT MY FAULT IF MONSTERS REALLY ARE EVERYWHERE!

THEY COULD BE RIGHT BEHIND YOU!
EEK!
MA'AM, YOU'RE SCARING MY DAD!
Live in fear!

AND, LAST BUT NOT LEAST, THE TEXAN TYCOON JOHNNY GALLON, ONE OF THE RICHEST MEN IN THE WORLD!
ON THIS WORLD, ANYWAY!
AHEM!
PIK-PIK

OOPS! HEH, HEH! I ALMOST FORGOT! ALSO BOUND FOR SPACE IS MR. MICKEY MOUSE!
THERE YOU ARE!
HOORAY! YOU'RE A CELEBRITY!

WE CHOSE HIM BECAUSE A GROUP MADE UP OF SUCH STAGGERINGLY FAMOUS PEOPLE ALSO NEEDS AN UTTERLY ORDINARY EVERYMAN!
!

OH...
GOSH...
SO YOU'RE NOT FAMOUS?

HA HA! GOTCHA!
YOU'RE WORTH A MILLION OF THOSE HOITY-TOITY VIPS!
SMACK

SEE YA TOMORROW AT THE LAUNCH!
ARE YOU NERVOUS AT ALL?
TO GO INTO SPACE? WHY WOULD I BE?

MICKEY, I MADE YOU A LITTLE SOMETHING FOR YOUR TRIP.
A SWEATER? WELL, THANKS, BUT...

...I DON'T THINK IT'LL GET VERY WINDY UP THERE!
NO, BUT THERE WILL BE STARS...AND STARLETS!

OH! I DON'T SUPPOSE THAT MEANS THE SWEATER...
IT MEANS YOU, HANDSOME!
PROPERTY OF MINNIE!

I DON'T WANT THAT BREAKHEARTS WOMAN GETTING ANY FUNNY IDEAS!
AW, SHUCKS, MINNIE!
SMUACK

AND DON'T BE NERVOUS, SWEETIE...YOU'LL BE FINE UP THERE! NOWADAYS, TRAVELING IN SPACE IS AS SAFE AS DRIVING A CAR!

P-THUMP
MINNIE! MY BUMPER!
OOPS! SORRY, HORACE!

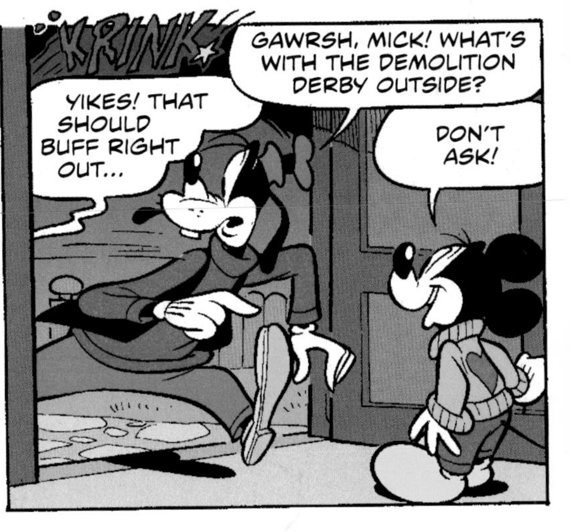
KRINK
YIKES! THAT SHOULD BUFF RIGHT OUT...
GAWRSH, MICK! WHAT'S WITH THE DEMOLITION DERBY OUTSIDE?
DON'T ASK!

I JUST SAW YUH ON THE TV, MICKEY! YUH *CAN'T* GO UP THERE TOMORROW!
AW, WHY NOT, GOOFY?

READ *THIS!* YOU COULD RUN INTO SCARY SPACE-MONSTERS HIDIN' BEHIND PLANETS OR IN YOUR CEREAL!
WIVES AN' TALES, GOOFY, THAT BOOK'S UNRELIABLE!
Cassandra Dot - Scary Ghosts in Deep Space

WAIT A SEC! AIN'T YUH NEVER HEARD OF THE SOLAR SPECTER?
I THINK YOU MEAN "SPECTRUM."

AT LEAST LET *ME* GO TOO! I'LL USE MY *BOOK-LEARNIN'* TO HELP YUH!
THANKS, BUT IT'S NOT UP TO ME! I'LL JUST BE A *GUEST!*

ƐGROAN!Ǝ DON'T SAY I DIDN'T WARN YUH, GHOST APOLOGIST. G'NIGHT!
G'NIGHT, GOOFY.

SO...
...SPACE GHOSTS! THEY CAN'T BE REAL...
...YEESH! THAT WOULD BE LIKE LIVING IN A *LIVING NIGHTMARE!*

THE NEXT DAY, CONCERNS ARE QUICKLY FORGOTTEN...
YOO-HOO! OVER HERE, MUSCLES!
ALL TOGETHER, PLEASE! FOR THE PRESS!
HMPH! WHAT A GAUDY OUTFIT.

NOW, MISS BREAKHEARTS, I'LL HAVE YOU KNOW THIS HANDSOME MOUSE HERE IS SPOKEN FOR!
HUH? WHO...OH!

NO WORRIES THERE, I PROMISE YOU!
...SINGLE?
VERY SINGLE!
!

NOW, HONEY, STAND UP STRAIGHT! SHE'LL NEVER NOTICE YOU LIKE THAT!
HOO BOY...!

LIFTOFF!
VO-OMMMMM

ATTENTION! WE'RE NOW LEAVING EARTH'S ATMOSPHERE! THE CAPTAIN WOULD LIKE TO WELCOME OUR GUESTS...

...AND INVITE YOU ALL TO ENJOY REFRESHMENTS IN THE PANORAMIC PAVILION!
WOW!
FUTILITY

THIS VIEW IS SO ROMANTIC! JUST LOOK AT ALL THE STARS OUT THERE!
THE CAPTAIN'S DOING A GREAT JOB AVOIDING THEM ALL!
HEH, HEH! THOSE TWO MAKE A FINE PAIR!

LOOKS LIKE MR. STARBUCK IS LOOKING FOR A PAIRING OF A DIFFERENT KIND...
...SO MANY REASONS OLYMPUS IS PRIME FOR INVESTMENT! THIS MONTH ALONE...
HMM...

LOOK ALIVE, MICKEY! WHO KNOWS WHAT'S AROUND HERE... UFOS, GHOSTS, SPACE AMOEBAS...WHO KNOWS WHAT'S IN STORE FOR US?
HUH?

A NICE VACATION, I HOPE!
DON'T PRETEND TO BE CALM! I KNOW YOU HAVE A LOVE OF MYSTERIES!

AREN'T YOU CURIOUS AS TO WHAT COULD BE OUT THERE IN DEEP SPACE?
WELL GOSH, OF COURSE I'M CURIOUS!

AHA! "AN UNCANNY SENSE OF DREAD FILLED THE SHIP! EVEN MICKEY MOUSE COULD FEEL IT!"
CLIC
HEY! I DIDN'T SAY THAT...!

MAYBE NOT VERBATIM, BUT DON'T DENY THAT'S HOW YOU TRULY FEEL!
"TRULY"? YOU KNOW, MISS DOT...

...HAVE YOU CONSIDERED WRITING SCIENCE FICTION NOVELS? IT SEEMS LIKE IT WOULDN'T BE MUCH OF A STRETCH FOR YOU!
!

HAVE YOU CONSIDERED MINDING YOUR OWN BUSINESS?
GUESS I COULD HAVE PUT THAT MORE TACTFULLY... SO MUCH FOR FIRST IMPRESSIONS!

YOUR ATTENTION, PLEASE! WE'RE READY TO DOCK AT THE FABULOUS *OLYMPUS HOTEL!*
COOOOL!
OOH!
AAAH!
SPECTACULAR!

PLEASE MAKE YOURSELVES COMFORTABLE AND ENJOY OUR FANTASTIC LUXURIES! WE HAVE A SAUNA, GYMS, POOLS... OLYMPUS IS ALL FOR YOU!

UGH...I HOPE THIS RECYCLED AIR DOESN'T CHAP MY LIPS! THEY'RE INSURED FOR A *MILLION DOLLARS!*
HEH...
HUH?
GROWL...

F-FUNNY! THAT GROWL SOUNDED LIKE IT CAME FROM...
...SOME KIND OF *BEAST!* BUT THAT'S IMPOSSIBLE... RIGHT?

LATER...
NICE HERE, ISN'T IT?
CAN'T BEAT THE VIEW! IT MIGHT EVEN BE WORTH AN INVESTMENT...

...AS LONG AS STARBUCK STOPS DROOLING OVER MY WALLET!
SPEAKING OF DROOLING, IT'S ABOUT TIME FOR DINNER!

WELL, WELL! GUESS WE'RE NEIGHBORS!
GUESS SO...
HUH?!
FLIP

WHAT IS IT? WHAT DID YOU SEE??
UH...NOTHING?
AM I LOSING IT??

AT DINNER...
THE MEAL'S DELICIOUS, MR. STARBUCK!
TYPICALLY I PREFER A GOOD OL' BURGER AND FRIES, BUT IN THIS CASE I AGREE!
THERE'S MUCH MORE WHERE THAT CAME FROM! OUR PANTRY IS BIG AND WELL-STOCKED!

BUT SUDDENLY...
AAAHH! DID YOU SEE THAT? OUT THERE! IT WAS A... A SHAPE!
GOOD GRAVY! NOT A SHAPE!

THUMP... THUMP THUMP...
LISTEN TO THAT! IT MUST BE A SECTOID BOARDING PARTY!
NONSENSE! THERE'S NOTHING TO FEAR! NOW WHO WANTS MOUSSE?

YOU CAN'T DENY THOSE ARE FOOTSTEPS!
NOW, I'M SURE IT'S ONLY ZOND, TAKING SOME READINGS...

GREETINGS, COMPATRIOTS! ER...IS SOMETHING AMISS?
!
EEEK! THERE IS SOMETHING OUT THERE!

ARE YOU CERTAIN YOU'RE NOT HALLUCINATING?
YES, INDEED! PERHAPS IT'S AUTO-SUGGESTION, OR--
STOP WITH THE HOGWASH! TELL US THE TRUTH!

SOMETHING IS OUT THERE! WE ALL HEARD IT; BELLA EVEN SAW IT! AND SO DID MICKEY...RIGHT?

WELL...YEAH, BUT I DON'T KNOW *WHAT...*

WHAT'S GOING ON HERE? I DEMAND *EASY ANSWERS!*
IN MY PROFESSIONAL ESTIMATION, WE'RE UNDER ATTACK FROM A HIGHLY DANGEROUS *SPACE CREATURE...*

...THAT LEAVES A *SLIMY TRAIL!*
OH, COME ON! NOW YOU'RE JUST BEING RIDICULOUS!

AM I? THEN HOW DO YOU EXPLAIN WHAT'S VERY CLEARLY A *SLIMY TRAIL?*
GASP!

WELL THAT TEARS IT! I AIN'T INVESTIN' IN NO HOTEL INFESTED WITH ALIENS!
GULP!

MY LIPS ARE CHAPPING FROM SCREAMING SO MUCH! YOU'RE GOING TO HEAR FROM MY TEAM OF LAWYERS!
NOW, C-CALM DOWN, PLEASE!

SOMEONE MUST ASSESS THIS SITUATION! I SHALL TAKE THE INITIATIVE!
BE CAREFUL!

I'M READY TO ACCEPT YOUR APOLOGY ANYTIME, MICKEY!
VOOOSH
ER...

PLEASE, EVERYONE, CALM DOWN! WE'LL SOLVE THE PROBLEM! NOW, WE'RE ABOUT TO BROADCAST TO EARTH, SO PLEASE LOOK PLEASANT AND DON'T THINK ABOUT ANY NASTY SPACE MONSTERS!
PSSST! STARBUCK!
?

LISTEN...BESIDES US, WHO ELSE IS ON BOARD?
THE COOK, TWO ATTENDANTS AND A TECHNICIAN! THEY CAME WITH US...

...AND ALL OF THEM ARE TRUSTWORTHY!
REALLY?
...HEY, YOU! WHAT ARE YOU DOING OVER THERE?
!

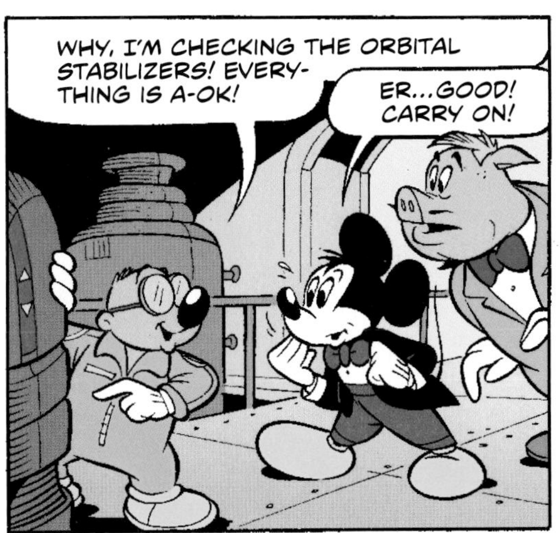
WHY, I'M CHECKING THE ORBITAL STABILIZERS! EVERY-THING IS A-OK!
ER...GOOD! CARRY ON!

WHAT'S IN YOUR HEAD, MICKEY?
WELL...ON ONE HAND, I FIND IT HARD TO BELIEVE IN A "SPACE MONSTER"...

...ON THE OTHER, IT'S CLEAR THAT SOMETHING IS OUT THERE! IT JUST HASN'T DONE ANYTHING TO HURT US!
THAT'S TRUE!

TELL THAT TO THE OTHER GUESTS - THAT MAY CALM THEM DOWN!
GOOD PLAN!

...GOT IT? IT DOESN'T WANT TO HURT US! SO SMILE NOW, BECAUSE WE'RE ABOUT TO BROADCAST LIVE! IS EVERYONE HERE?
ZOND HASN'T COME BACK YET...

--AND HERE WE ARE! SO, HOW IS THE *SPACE-CATION* GOING, EVERYONE?
HEH, HEH! WE'RE SURE HAVING FUN!

GREAT! SAY, MR. STARBUCK, WON'T YOU LET US SEE THE WONDERFUL *VIEW* FROM YOUR WINDOWS?
OH! BUT OF COURSE!

I DARESAY THE VIEW WE HAVE WILL LEAVE YOU SPEECHLESS!
...VRRR
RRR...

I SEE...THOUGH I WOULDN'T SAY "SPEECHLESS" IS THE FIRST WORD THAT COMES TO MIND...
?!?

AAAAAAAAAAAHH!

TARNATION! "DOESN'T WANT TO HURT US", INDEED!
IT'S TOO MUCH...!
OFF! TURN IT OFF! GO TO COMMERCIALS!

MICKEY! TH-THAT WRITING...IT LOOKS LIKE IT WAS CARVED WITH A CLAW!
I-I'M SURE THERE'S A PERFECTLY RATIONAL EXPLANATION...!

ZOND! YOU WERE OUTSIDE! DID YOU SEE WHO WROTE THAT?
I...
I...

I SAW...WELL...WHAT I SAW DEFIES DESCRIPTION!

"WHEN ZOND RETURNED HE WAS PALE, AS IF HE HAD SEEN A GHOST!"
A GHOST?? OH MY...
CLIC
OH, PLEASE!

YOU'D BETTER COME WITH ME, MISS DOT, BEFORE YOU DO ANY MORE DAMAGE TO THE EASILY CONFUSED!

YOU CAN'T GO AROUND FUELING PEOPLE'S FEARS JUST TO SELL MORE BOOKS!
"MICKEY BLAMED MY JOURNALISM SKILLS INSTEAD OF FACING FACTS!"
CLIC

AW, FORGET IT! GO DO WHAT YOU LIKE!
WAIT...DON'T LEAVE!

WHATEVER YOU MAY THINK OF ME, SOMETHING'S WRONG! AND WE HAVE TO GET TO THE BOTTOM OF IT!
I KNOW!

THAT DOES IT! IF YOU WON'T LISTEN TO ME, THEN I'LL JUST HAVE TO CHANGE MY TUNE!
?

I REALLY DO WANT TO FIND OUT THE *TRUTH!* EVEN IF IT MEANS IGNORING MY OWN THEORIES AND HELPING *YOU* SOLVE THE MYSTERY INSTEAD!
WOW, I, UH... REALLY?

ATTENTION, EVERYONE! MICKEY IS RIGHT: THERE'S NOTHING TO FEAR! WHATEVER IS OUT THERE CAN'T COME INSIDE! WE'RE *SAFE!*

ASTUTELY PUT!
DARN TOOTIN'! SHE IS THE EXPERT!
RIGHT!
?

HOW DID I DO?
GREAT! NOW THE BEST THING TO DO IS GET SOME REST. WE CAN'T THINK WITH FRAYED NERVES.

BUT LATER...
I CAN'T SEEM TO RELAX!
BUT...
MAYBE SOME CLASSICAL MUSIC IS WHAT I NEED! JUST NEED TO... UNWIND A LITTLE...

!!!
ALARM!
HOW RELAXING...
WEEEEE

I'M SO RELAXED IT FEELS LIKE I'M SINKING...
ALARM!
WEEEEEEEE

WAIT--ROCKS AN' STONES! I AM SINKING!

ACK! AND NOW I'M FLYING! WHAT'S GOING ON??
LARM!

MICKEY! HAVEN'T YOU HEARD?
WE HAVE TO ABANDON SHIP! IMMEDIATELY!
WEEEEEE

THE ORBITAL STABILIZERS HAVE BEEN DESTROYED! THE OLYMPUS HAS FALLEN INTO A SPIRALING ORBIT WHICH MEANS...
I'M RUINED!

...IT'S GOING TO DISINTEGRATE IN EARTH'S ATMOSPHERE!
AND I'M RUINED!

THESE RESCUE PODS SHOULD TAKE US SAFELY TO EARTH!
WHAT ABOUT THE SPACE SHUTTLE?

IT'S BEEN DAMAGED BY ALL THE GRAVITY FLUCTUATION! SHODDY CRAFTSMANSHIP, IF YOU ASK ME! NOW GO FIND A POD!
SOB!
FZUP

ALSO: THE STABILIZERS LOOK LIKE THEY WERE SABOTAGED! I SUSPECT THAT "THING," WHATEVER IT IS... IS IN HERE!
GASP!

UH...WHAT'S WITH ALL THE CLOTHES?
OH, NO...

OH, DEAR! I THOUGHT YOU HAD ALL LEFT ALREADY, SO I FILLED ALL THE PODS WITH MY WARDROBE! I'M SURE YOU UNDERSTAND!
!!!

I'LL DEDICATE MY NEXT AWARD TO YOUUUUUUUUU!
NO! WE...WE'RE TRAPPED!
FZUP

MAYBE NOT! LET'S CHECK OUT THE SHUTTLE...EVEN IF IT DOESN'T WORK PERFECTLY...
HANGAR
OIL

...WE MAY AT LEAST BE ABLE TO GET OFF THE OLYMPUS AND SEND AN S.O.S. ONCE WE'RE IN SPACE!

WHEW! THE CONTROLS STILL WORK!
HUH?

M-MICKEY... LOOK AT THIS!
GASP! THE ALIEN IS ON BOARD...WITH **US!**
LIFE FORMS ON BOARD:
3

IT'S IN THE STORAGE COMPARTMENT! CASSANDRA, YOU STAY HERE, I'LL GO TAKE CARE OF THIS.
NO WAY! I WANT TO SEE THIS FOR MYSELF!

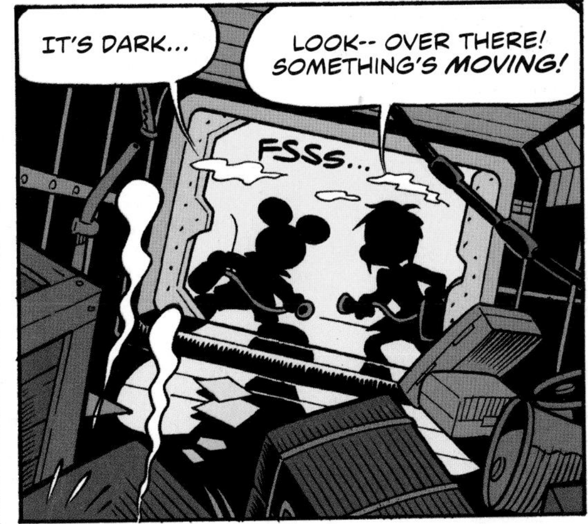
IT'S DARK...
LOOK-- OVER THERE! SOMETHING'S **MOVING!**
FSSS...

URGHHHH....
ALRIGHT! ON THE COUNT OF 3, WE **SPRAY** IT!
GHOOF

AAAAH! TOO LATE!!
WAIT! B-BUT THAT'S...!

HYUK! HOWDY, FELLERS!
...GOOFY! WHAT ARE YOU DOING HERE?
F-FRIEND OF YOURS?

GAWRSH, I JUST WANTED TO PROTECT YA, MICK! SO I STOWED AWAY IN A SUITCASE THAT WAS WAY TOO SMALL!

SO THIS IS THE MONSTER WE ALL HEARD?
I DOUBT IT. WHAT'S YOUR STORY, GOOFY?

"I WANTED TO STAY HIDDEN, BUT IT WEREN'T LONG BEFORE I GOT A-RUMBLY IN MUH TUMMY..."
?
GROOOWL

"SO I HEADED FER THE PANTRY ROOM - FROM THE OUTSIDE, SO I WOULDN'T BE SEEN!"

"BUT THAT WENT OVER LIKE A BAG OF WET SNAKES! I FORGOT ALL ABOUT MUH PESKY SHADOW!"
AAAAAH!
GULP!
CHIPS

AND THOSE WERE YOUR FOOTSTEPS! YOU REALLY SCARED US!
HYUK! *YOU* WERE SCARED? I WAS SO NERVOUS...

"...I DROPPED MUH ONLY JAR OF GRAPE JELLY!"

GAWRSH!
AHA! THERE'S YOUR "SLIME TRAIL!"

DON'T LAUGH JUST YET! YOUR STORY DOESN'T EXPLAIN WHY WE'RE ***PLUMMETING TOWARDS EARTH!***
HUH?

SOMEBODY SABOTAGED OLYMPUS! AND I DOUBT IT WAS WITH GRAPE JELLY!
WE NEED TO GET OUT OF HERE!
AW HECK, I'D HELP YOU FELLERS, BUT ORBITAL TELEMETRY AIN'T MUH STRONG SUIT!

OOOF!
RRRUMBLE
?!

WHAT... WHAT WAS THAT?

LOOK! I THINK-- I THINK WE'VE STOPPED!
GREAT! THE STABILIZERS MUST BE WORKING AGAIN!

WAITASEC... THEY COULDN'T HAVE JUST FIXED THEMSELVES!
B-BUT...
GULP! YOU'RE SAYING...

SOMEBODY ELSE DID!
WE'D BETTER GO SEE!

GAWRSH, IT'S QUIET!
SHH!

OVER THERE! LOOK!
W-WHO IS THAT?
CLOP CLOP

ZOND! BUT... CAPES AN' COWLS! IT WAS ONLY A MASK!
I KNEW IT! ZOND IS REALLY AN ALIEN!

GULP! NO--
WORSE!

OBSTINATE VERMIN! YOU SHOULD HAVE LONG VACATED THE PREMISES!
PHANTOM BLOT!

HYUK! SO YOU'VE BEEN BREAKIN' AND FIXIN'!
WHO ELSE COULD DEVISE SUCH AN INGENIOUS INGRESS? DON'T MOVE, OR RISK THE WRATH OF MY STUN GUN!

I THOUGHT ZOND HAD A FAMILIAR VOCABULARY!
MY SINGLE SHORTCOMING, ALAS: I FIND IT IMPOSSIBLE TO OBSCURE MY INTELLECT!

BUT EVEN THAT DID NOT IMPEDE AN OTHERWISE EXCEPTIONAL STRATAGEM: TO CONVINCE ALL ABOARD THE OLYMPUS TO ABANDON SHIP!
?

"AN ADMITTED WRINKLE GREW APPARENT WHEN YOU FANCIFUL FOOLS CONCLUDED AN ALIEN HAD COME ABOARD!"
?

"I COULDN'T RISK INTERFERENCE--EXTRATERRESTRIAL OR OTHERWISE--SO I WENT TO INVESTIGATE!"
SOMEONE MUST ASSESS THIS SITUATION!

TSK! FRIGHTENED BY A *CONDIMENT!* NO DOUBT CAST OFF FROM THIS TRASH CHUTE!

"USING MY FINELY-TUNED IMPROVISATIONAL ACUMEN, I TOOK ADVANTAGE OF YOUR PARANOIA!"
HMM...

THIS SHOULD SEND THOSE NERVOUS NINNIES CRYING HOME TO MOMMY!
SKRSSK

BUT WHY, PHANTOM BLOT? I DON'T PEG YOU FOR A REAL ESTATE MOGUL!
GAWRSH, MAYBE HE JUST NEEDS HIS OWN *SPACE?*
A SALIENT POINT, FRIEND, HOWEVER POORLY WORDED!

THE TRUTH OF THE MATTER IS THAT THE OLYMPUS IS *NOT* A HOTEL AT ALL!
?!?

"WHEN STARBUCK HIRED ZOND FOR THE OLYMPUS PROJECT, I IMMEDIATELY REPLACED HIM!"

?
GREETINGS!
Z

"IT WAS THEN CHILD'S PLAY TO CONVINCE STARBUCK'S TECHNICIANS TO FOLLOW MY DESIGNS!"
IT'S QUITE A PIECE OF WORK, MR. ZOND!
THE BEST IS YET TO COME, MR. STARBUCK!

"AND IF SOMEONE GOT TOO CURIOUS..."
SIR, WHY ARE WE INSTALLING A 16-MEGA-TON LASER CANNON IN THE PRESIDENTIAL SUITE?
WHY, FOLLOW ME AND I'LL SHOW YOU!
STARB

"...I ENGINEERED THEIR *DISAPPEARANCE!*"
!
POKK
STARBUC
NO! ALL THOSE INNOCENT WORKERS...

"DO NOT FRET; THEY'VE GONE TO A WARMER PLACE!"
HEY, A NEW ARRIVAL!
ABOUT TIME! NOW WE HAVE ENOUGH FOR HEARTS!

BUT ONLY NOW CAN I TAKE *POSSESSION* OF OLYMPUS...AND FINALLY FULFILL AN OLD DREAM!
CLONK
OLYMPUS
ALTERNATE CONFIGURATION

BEHOLD, SIMPLETONS! GAZE UPON THE TRUE FACE OF...
!
!!
VZRKRR
VZRRRRR....
TZ-CLOCK

...OLYMPUS, THE ORBITING NIGHTMARE!

LIKE MIGHTY ZEUS, I SHALL HURL THUNDER ACROSS THE EARTH AND FORCE OBEISANCE FROM HUMANITY!
ZOT ZOT
!

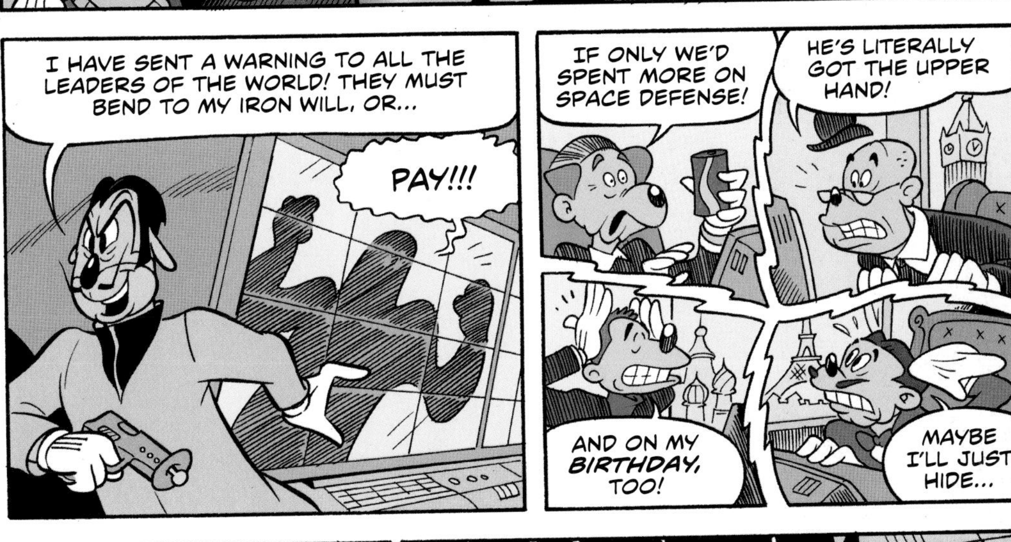
I HAVE SENT A WARNING TO ALL THE LEADERS OF THE WORLD! THEY MUST BEND TO MY IRON WILL, OR...
PAY!!!
IF ONLY WE'D SPENT MORE ON SPACE DEFENSE!
HE'S LITERALLY GOT THE UPPER HAND!
AND ON MY *BIRTHDAY*, TOO!
MAYBE I'LL JUST HIDE...

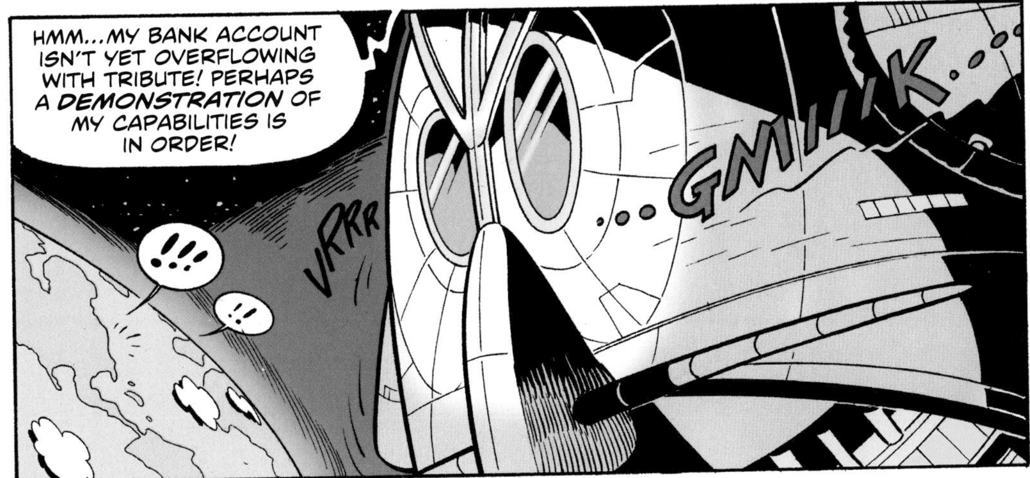
HMM...MY BANK ACCOUNT ISN'T YET OVERFLOWING WITH TRIBUTE! PERHAPS A *DEMONSTRATION* OF MY CAPABILITIES IS IN ORDER!
...GMIIIK...
VRRR
!!!
!!

THE FIRST TARGET SHALL BE MOUSETON! I NEVER DID CARE FOR THE TRAFFIC...
TARGET ACQUIRED! COMPLETE ANNIHILATION IN 10...9...

NOOO!!!
YOU CAN'T DO THIS!!
ERGH...

KEEP QUIET, YOU AURAL OFFENDERS, OR I'LL STUN YOU INTO THE NEXT MILLENNIUM!
GULP!

G-GOSH, WE DON'T MEAN NO HARM! I JUST WANT TO... APOLOGIZE TO GOOFY!
HUH? FER WHAT, MICK?
PAT PAT

FOR... THIS!
BOOSTER
VOOOOOSH
GAWRRRSH!
ACK!
CLIC

HEADS UP!
WHOOF!

GOOFY, YOU GOTTA STOP THAT LASER BEAM!
SHUCKS, FIRST I GOTTA STOP MYSELF!
5...4...3...

2...1...FIRE!
TZOTT

IT...HIT THE SEA!
THE LASER MUST NOT BE CARBURATED YET!
FUPP...

INDEED, MY PROJECTIONS WERE FAULTY...
POK
!
TZUT
STOCK
...BUT I'LL HAVE AMPLE TIME TO RECALCULATE ONCE I'VE STUNNED YOU INTERLOPERS INTO SUBMISSION!

?
BUT... WHAT...?
FLIP

THE STUN GUN SHOT A HOLE IN THE WINDOW! SHODDY CRAFTSMANSHIP *INDEED!*
OH, NOOO!
SVVVUUUUUU

URGH!
T-P-BUK

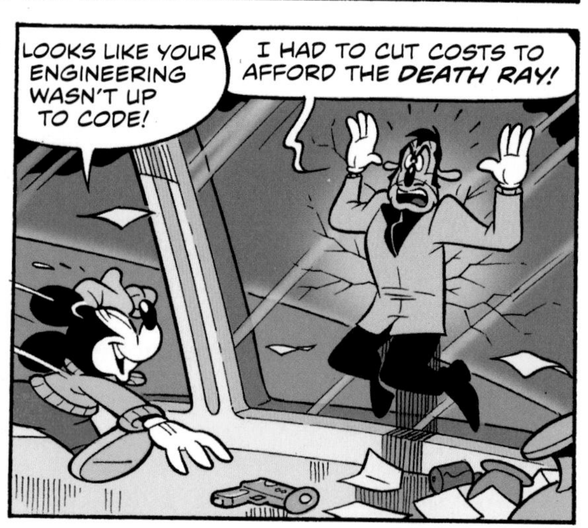
LOOKS LIKE YOUR ENGINEERING WASN'T UP TO CODE!
I HAD TO CUT COSTS TO AFFORD THE *DEATH RAY!*

ER...HELLO? ABOUT THAT THREAT OF YOURS...
DO YOU ACCEPT PERSONAL CHECKS?
!

DON'T WORRY! EVERYTHING'S OK, GUYS! BUT WE COULD SURE USE A RESCUE, AND THE BLOT HERE COULD USE SOME *JAIL TIME!*
GRRR!

AND SO, THE RETURN TO MOUSETON IS TRIUMPHANT!
THIS IS THE STORY OF THE YEAR!
THERE HE IS!
MICKEY, OVER HERE!
TELL US EVERYTHING!
AND I DO MEAN EVERY-THING!
MBC

WELL, IT ALL STARTED WHEN THE PHANTOM BLOT DISGUISED HIM-SELF AS--
WHAT? NO, NO!
WE MEAN...

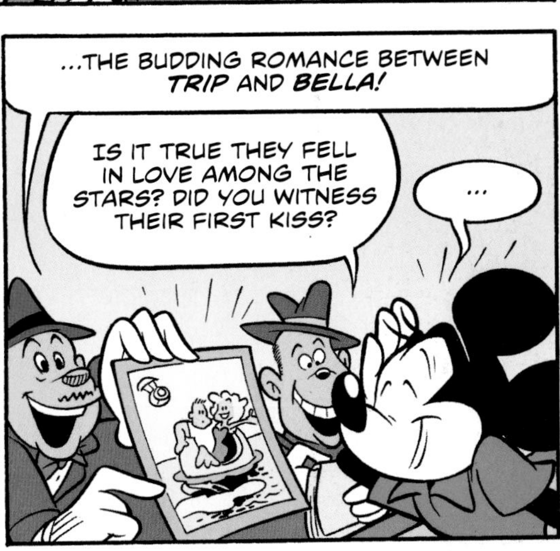
...THE BUDDING ROMANCE BETWEEN TRIP AND BELLA!
IS IT TRUE THEY FELL IN LOVE AMONG THE STARS? DID YOU WITNESS THEIR FIRST KISS?
...

JOURNALISTS NEVER CHANGE!
WELL, I'D SAY ONE OF THEM CHANGED...RIGHT, CASSANDRA?
YOU REALLY THINK SO, MICKEY?

I'LL WRITE IN MY BOOK HOW SMART AND BRAVE YOU WERE...AND IT WON'T BE SCIENCE FICTION!
SHUCKS!
SMACK

OH, GREAT! I KNEW YOU'D GET IN TROUBLE IF YOU TOOK THE SWEATER OFF!
SORRY, MINNIE...IT JUST FITS THE PHANTOM BLOT BETTER!
GRRR!

IF YOU ONLY KNEW HOW WORRIED I WAS!
SHE'S GOT A WORRY ROOM OF HER OWN NOW!

YOU MUST HAVE SO MANY GREAT STORIES TO TELL US!
I MIGHT HAVE A FEW...
STARS, SPACE MONSTERS...

NAW! WE DIDN'T SEE ANY GHOSTS OR MONSTERS OR EVEN CREEPY-CRAWLIES! SPACE AIN'T SO SCARY AFTER ALL!
HUH?
TOO BAD...

...BUT WE HOPE YOU'LL ENJOY A DOWN-TO-EARTH PARTY ANYWAY! WELCOME HOME!
WELCOME HOME MICKEY!
MICKEY
THE END!

MICKEY MOUSE
in The
MENACE FROM THE FUTURE!
WALT DISNEY

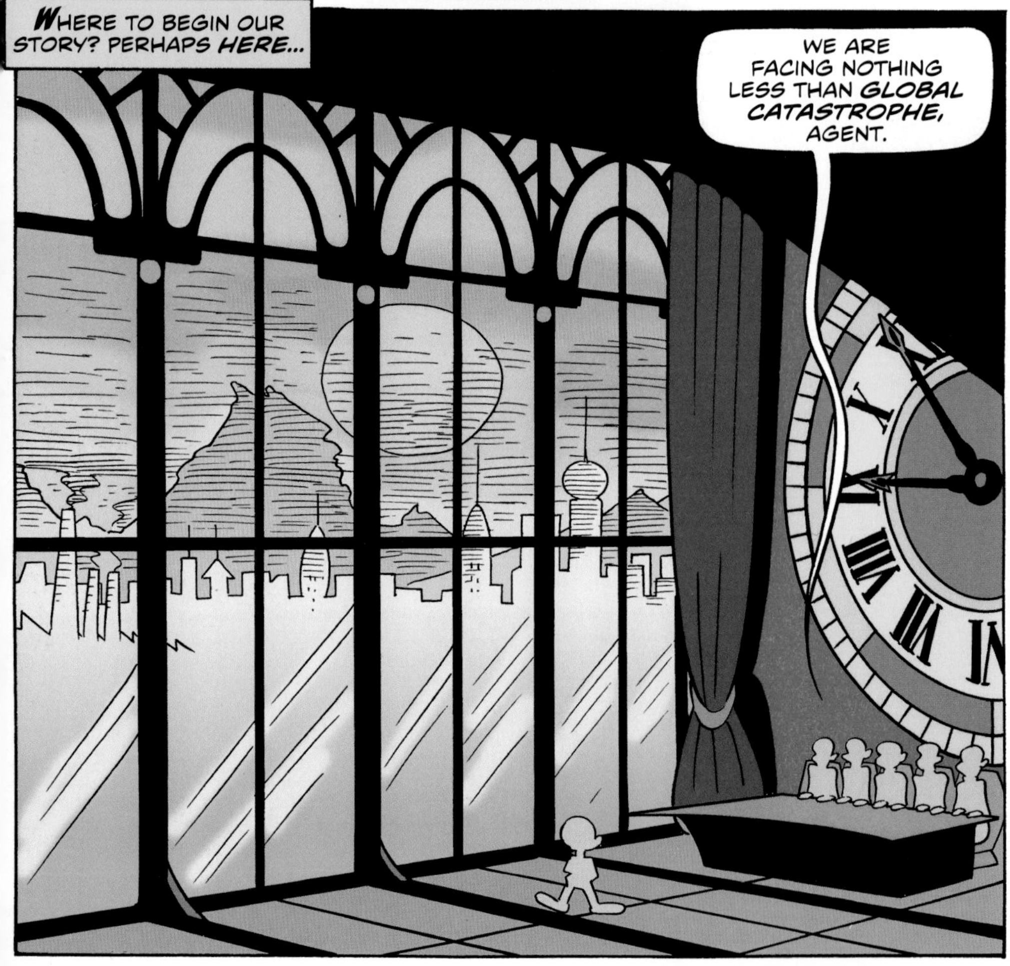
WHERE TO BEGIN OUR STORY? PERHAPS HERE...
WE ARE FACING NOTHING LESS THAN GLOBAL CATASTROPHE, AGENT.

YOU MUST FIND THOSE WHO ARE KNOWN AS "THE BUBBLEBRAINS!" DEAL WITH THEM...PERMANENTLY!
AND DO NOT RETURN WITHOUT THEIR LEADER...

...THE GRIM GAGAGOOFY, DESTROYER OF WORLDS!

THERE IS NO MARGIN FOR ERROR!
WITH ALL OF EARTH HANGING IN THE BALANCE...
...YOU ARE OUR ONE HOPE...

...OUR BEST HOPE...AND OUR LAST HOPE!
GOOD LUCK, AND GOOD HUNTING...

...AGENT UMA!

A MISTY, MOISTY EVENING-- ELSEWHERE!
DOOFUS B. DAWG
THANKS FER THE BUGGY RIDE, FELLERS! HYEK! YUH REALLY THINK I DON'T NEED TA WORRY?
NAW! COUSIN MOOFY'S JUST GOIN' THROUGH A ROUGH PATCH, PROBABLY!

HE'S RIGHT! AIN'T NOTHIN' TO BE SCARED OF BUT THE WIDENING POVERTY GAP AN' GOBLIN MONKEYS!

GOOD EVENING.
EVENIN' YERSELF, MA'AM! HYEK! DO I KNOW YUH FROM SOMEWHERES?

YOU MIGHT SAY THAT! YOU ARE A BUBBLE-BRAIN...CORRECT?
ALWAYS HAVE BEEN! WHUT CAN I DO FOR YUH?

MORE THAN YOU WOULD EVER BELIEVE.
SAY! CAREFUL WITH THAT THERE--

THE NEXT MORNING...
HMM... HUMAN INTEREST TIME ON KWAK-TV!
...AND NOW THE LATEST ON OUR HYPNO-MAN!
KWAK TV

AREA RESIDENT DOOFUS B. DAWG SEEMS TO BE IN A TRANCE, THINKING HE'S A KANGAROO FROM TIMBUKTU! TEE-HEE!
HONK!
KWAK TV

GOSH, BILL, DOES THIS GUY NEED A SHRINK...OR A GPS?
MUST BE SWEEPS WEEK...KWAK'S WORKING HARD TO AVOID REAL STORIES!

ALL THIS TALK OF TRANCES AND HYPNOSIS REMINDS ME OF ANOTHER STORY I JUST READ IN THE--

--PAPER! WAIT A SEC...
MONITOR
LOCAL MAN CONVINCED HE IS HUMAN AIRPLANE
Moofus P. Dawg: "I Believe I Can

...I KNOW THOSE TWO KOOKS! THEY'RE DOOFY AND MOOFY, COUSINS OF GOOFY!
DOOFUS B. DAWG

MAYBE I SHOULD ASK HIM WHAT THIS HYPNO-THING'S ABOUT? HOPE IT'S AS INNOCENT AS IT LOOKS...

HUH! GOOD TIMING!
BRRING! BRRING!
GOOFY
GOOFY

HEY, GOOFY, GUESS WHO I JUST SAW ON TV--
NO TIME FOR CELEBRITY TALK, MICK! I NEED YER HELP!

I'M IN A REAL HIGHFALUTIN' HUMDINGER! COME QUI-- CLICK!
?!

SHEESH! WHY AM I SUDDENLY GETTING A BAD FEELING ABOUT THIS?
113

AND WHAT...WHAT'S HE DONE TO HIS HOUSE??
BubbleBrains H.Q.
KEEP OUT!
TOP KRUT
GOOFY

COR! NOW JUST A TAD MORE SALT...
NAW, YUH WANT SUGAR, YUH GALOOT!
EASY, FELL-ERS!
ARGUIN'S AGAINST THUH PRINCIPLES OF--
TOP SEKRUT

GOWRSH! DO WE HIDE, OR ANSWER THE DOOR?
I'LL HIDE, YOU ANSWER!
NOK NOK

WHO GOES THERE?
UH...I'M MICKEY! IS GOOFY IN?

I SAY, GOOFUS, DO YOU KNOW A LAD NAMED HICKEY?
HMMM...CAN'T SAY I DO!
A-HA!
GO AWAY

A SPY, I'D WAGER!
I KNOWED SOMEONE'D WANNA STEAL OUR SMART IDEARS!
?
TLAK

SOMETHING'S HAPPENING HERE...BUT WHAT IT IS AIN'T EXACTLY CLEAR!
GIT LOST

IF I GOTTA BE NOSY, I GOTTA BE--
HUH?
GUWRSH! THUH SPY'S GOTTEN THROUGH OUR SECURITY!
IT'S OK, COUSINS! THIS HERE'S MUH PAL! WELCOME TA BUBBLEBRAIN CENTRAL, MICK!

THIS HERE'S MUH COUSIN TOOFUS...
CALL ME TOOFY FER SHORT! HYIK!

DOGUE-BERRY, SIR! I 'AVEN'T GOT A NICKNAME. HYOK!
HE'S MUH COUSIN FROM FUNNY-TALKIN' ENGLAND!

WE'VE ASSEMBLED THE WHOLE FAMILY TA INVENT THUH WORLD'S WILDEST SODY POP!
I HEARD ABOUT THAT CONTEST! DEADLINE'S TOMORROW, RIGHT?
TESTS

BLOODY WELL RIGHT! AND OUR ENTRY'S NEARLY DONE!
WE COULD WIN TEN MILLION SMACKERS IN CASH!

PURPLE RAIN PUNCH! A TEMPTING TICKLE TO YOUR TASTEBUDS, GOV'NOR!

IT'S ALMOST READY!
AN' ALMOST TASTES GOOD, TOO! WANNA SIP?
IT SURE LOOKS NICE AND SPARKLY...

BUT...
THAT EGGPLANT FLAVOR...

TOLDJA! IT TAKES A SPOONFUL O' SUGAR TA MAKE THUH EGGPLANT GO DOWN!
IT NEEDS SALT, MAN! SALT!
WE SHOULDA USED MUSTARD!

GOOFY... THIS CAN'T BE THE CRISIS YOU CALLED ME ABOUT.
HECK, NO. THAT'D BE THUH FELLER WHO'S MUTATIN' OUR MINDS. HYUK!

AYE! AND A MIND IS A TERRIBLE THING TO MUTATE!
WE CALL HIM THE DE-BUBBLER! WE AIN'T SEEN WHUT HE LOOKS LIKE, BUT WE KNOW WHUT HE CAN DO!
?!

COUSIN DOOFY MET THUH FELLER LAST NIGHT! AN' EVER SINCE--
HONK!
HONK!

SEE? HYPNERTIZED AN' USELESS! AN' HE WAS IN CHARGE OF MARKETING!
VOOOM

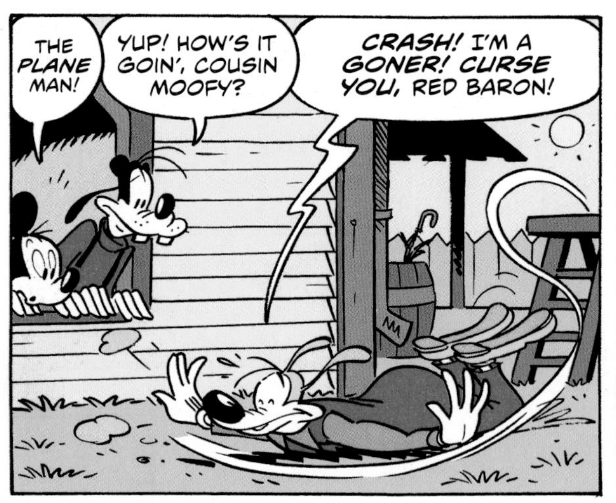
THE PLANE MAN!
YUP! HOW'S IT GOIN', COUSIN MOOFY?
CRASH! I'M A GONER! CURSE YOU, RED BARON!

I CURSE THE DE-BUBBLER... WHOEVER 'E IS!
THAT DURN PEG-LEG PETE, I BET!
?

PETE'S ENTERIN' THUH CONTEST, TOO! HE'D DO ANYTHING TA WIN... EVEN HYPNERTIZE US!

THAT FELLER AIN'T ABOVE BOARD! HE DON'T CARE NONE FER SODY-POP...
...HE JUST WANTS THUH CASH PRIZE!
HMM...

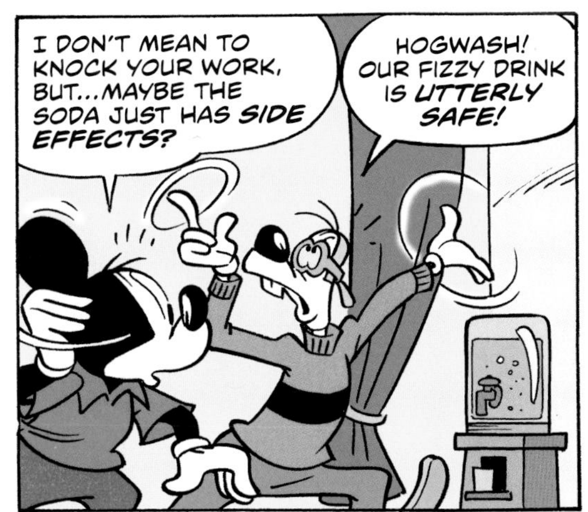
I DON'T MEAN TO KNOCK YOUR WORK, BUT...MAYBE THE SODA JUST HAS SIDE EFFECTS?
HOGWASH! OUR FIZZY DRINK IS UTTERLY SAFE!

AFTER ALL, WE THREE 'AVE DRUNK IT--
AN' WE'RE AS NORMAL AS PIGS IN A TREE!
OF... COURSE!

WELL...I'LL SEE IF PETE'S UP TO ANYTHING. KEEP A LOW PROFILE WHILE I'M GONE!
BubbleBrains H.Q.
GOOFY

REALLY, GOOFUS! MR. MOUSE MEANS WELL, BUT...
JUST TH' IDEAR OF PURPLE RAIN HAVIN' SIDE EFFECTS! HYIK!
HMM...

WHAT ABOUT PEG-LEG PETE, INDEED? LET'S CHECK IN AND SEE...

PHEW! MY CROOKA-COLA'S TOO STINKY TO WIN A CONTEST! BUT YOU KNOW WHAT THEY SAY...WINNING AIN'T EVERYTHING!
MILK

ALL I CARE ABOUT IS ENTERIN' AN' LOOKIN' LEGIT...SO THE JUDGES DON'T GUESS MY SODA JUG'S GOT A FALSE BOTTOM!
POP

THAT'S WHERE I'LL HIDE THE PRIZE MONEY AFTER I SWIPE IT! AN' I'LL BE ON A PLANE TO THEMBRIA BEFORE ANYONE GETS WISE!

HMM...I'LL CONFRONT HIM FACE-TO-FACE...BUT I WON'T MENTION HYPNOTISM! IF HE DOES, THEN I'VE GOT HIM!

EVENING, PETE! SAY GOODNIGHT TO YOUR EVIL PLANS, ONCE AGAIN!
GAH! HOW'D YOU KN-- ER, PLANS? WHAT PLANS?!

COME ON. YOU WANT TO SABOTAGE GOOFY'S TEAM IN THE SODA CONTEST!
HUH?
OH!

HAH! YOU GOT ME WRONG, PAL! THOSE GUYS HAVE THE TASTE BUDS OF TERMITES! THEY AIN'T EVEN REAL COMPETITION!

UNLESS YOU THINK THOSE BUBBLEBRAINS GOT SOME ACTUAL SODA-MAKIN' TALENT?
ER...DEFINE "TALENT."

SEE? SO THERE AIN'T NO REASON TO SABOTAGE THEM! NOW QUIT TRYIN' TA FRAME ME AN' SCRAM!
FINE, FINE! SEE YA, PETE...

HMM...BUT IF SOMEONE IS SABOTAGIN' 'EM, MAYBE THERE'S A GOOD REASON I AIN'T HEARD OF...

MAYBE THEY'VE GOT SOMETHING WORTH INVESTIGATING... OR LIBERATING!

HEY! THAT'S NOT MUCH OF A LOW PROFILE, FELLAS!
GAWRSH, WE WAS HUNGRY! WE FIGGERED WE'D BE SAFE WHILE YUH KEPT THUH DE-BUBBLER BUSY!

I DON'T THINK PETE IS THE DE-BUBBLER! AND WHERE'S DOGUEBERRY--
?
DING-DING! WHOO!

FOR GOSH SAKES!
AW HECK! NOW DOGUEBERRY THINKS HE'S A TRAIN!
WHOO!
WHOOO!

CHUG!
CHUG!
AN' THAT AIN'T THUH HALF OF IT! LOOK!
!

OUR PURPLE RAIN SUPPLY'S BUSTED!
?!

LUCKY I STILL GOT THUH RECIPE UP HERE!
THIS CAN'T HAVE BEEN PETE! I WAS WITH HIM THE WHOLE TIME! BUT WHO...

WHO COULD CARE THIS MUCH ABOUT KNOCKING GOOFY AND HIS EGGPLANT SODA OUT OF THE CONTEST?
GUWRSH! WHUT NOW, MR. MOUSE?

PACK YOUR GEAR AND LEAVE SOME FOOD OUT FOR YOUR COUSINS! WE'RE MOVING YOU TWO TO A SAFER LOCATION...

...AT LEAST, I HOPE MY HOUSE IS SAFER!

WE CAN'T SLEEP, MICK! WE GOT CARBONATED NERVES!
TRY TO RELAX, PALS. I'M STANDING GUARD FOR YA! IF A HYPNOTIST DOES SHOW UP...
MORTY
FERDIE

...I'M READY TO PLAY A FEW HEAD GAMES, MY-SELF!

BUT THE NIGHT SEEMS CALM AND UNEVENTFUL...

YAWN! DOGGONE, I DOZED OFF! HOPE GOOFY AND TOOFY ARE OKAY...!

GZZZ!
ZAWP!
HEH! LOOK AT 'EM... SNUG AS BIG, DIPPY BUGS IN A RUG!

THOUGH I DIDN'T SLEEP SO WELL IN THAT CHAIR! I'LL BREW SOME COFFEE AN'-

DING-DONG!
HUH. 'S THAT THE MAILMAN? KINDA EARLY...

ACE POLLING COMPANY OF WALLA-WALLA, WASHINGTON! WHAT'S YOUR FAVORITE CHEESE, SIR?
?

CAMEB-- CAMBEMBER-- UH...SWISS?
FINE, IF A BIT PEDESTRIAN! NOW, MAY I ASK WHICH KIND YOUR TWO GUESTS PREFER?

ONE NEVER CAN TELL WITH CHEESE.
WAIT... "GUESTS?" HOW'D SHE KNOW I'VE GOT--

GOOD GRAVY! IS SHE THE DE-BUBBLER??
UH...N-NO GUESTS HERE! MY NEPHEWS ARE HOME AT MY SISTER'S--

HYIK! SLEEP WELL, MICKEY? BETTER START RE-MAKIN' THAT PURPLE RAIN PUNCH!
!
UH OH!

TOOFY! LOOK-- OW!
HUFF!
WHAM

HOLD IT RIGHT THERE, BUBBLEBRAIN!

!
TAKE THIS, YOU HATRACK!
ZATT
TOOFY! NO!!

I-AM-A-HATRACK! HYIK!
HYPNOTIZED! SO THAT'S HOW IT'S DONE!

EXCUSE THE BAD MANNERS, LADY! BUT Y'LEAVE ME NO OTHER...

...CHOICE?!
SVIPP

SPILL IT, MOUSE! WHERE'S THE LAST BUBBLEBRAIN-- AND THE GRIM GAGAGOOFY, DESTROYER OF WORLDS?
?!

HMPH! MY PAL'S NAME IS GOOFY! HE AIN'T THAT GRIM, AND "DESTROYER OF WORLDS" IS PRETTY HARSH FOR SOMEONE WHO'S JUST CLUMSY!
HUH?

IF YOU DON'T START MAKING SENSE, I'LL ZAP YOU, T--
SORRY! NO MORE HYPNERTIZIN' ALLOWED!
BONK!

SOON!
GAWRSH, I HADDA DO SOMETHIN' OR ELSE...
...SHE MIGHT HAVE ZAPPED US BOTH, I KNOW! BUT SHE SEEMS OK...
UGH...

SORRY ABOUT THAT, MISS, BUT YOU OWE US SOME ANSWERS! WHO ARE YOU, AND WHAT'S UP WITH THIS?
SIGH...MY NAME IS UMA. SPECIAL AGENT UMA!

A SPY HERE TA STEAL OUR SODA! I KNEW IT!
WHAT? NO...I'M HERE TO SAVE MY PEOPLE... THE PEOPLE OF MOUSETON...
?

...OR, REALLY, THE ENTIRE WORLD...OF 2049!
WHA??
BONK!

LADY, THAT BUMP ON YOUR HEAD MAY BE WORSE THAN WE THOUGHT!
YEAH, YOU DON'T BELIEVE ME, I GET IT...

...BUT MAYBE THIS SELF-PLAYING OMNIDISC WILL MAKE THINGS CLEAR!
CLIC

WHOA!
≯BZZT!≮ SEARCHING TIME...SEARCHING FOR TIMELINE OF EVENTS LEADING TO POWER SEIZURE BY THE GRIM GAGAGOOFY!
VOINN...
1999
2001
2007

ACCORDING TO HISTORICAL RECORDS, GAGAGOOFY FIRST SURFACED IN MOUSETON, CALISOTA IN THE YEAR 2010.
MOUSETON
2010

WITH THE HELP OF A TEAM OF EVIL SCIENTISTS NAMED THE BUBBLEBRAINS, HE PATENTED PURPLE RAIN, A SUPER-RENEWABLE ENERGY SOURCE.
GAGAGOOFY
TEAM BUBBLEBRAIN

THE PATENT MADE WORLDWIDE NEWS. ONE JAR OF PURPLE RAIN COULD FUEL A GAS VEHICLE FOR MONTHS.
PURPLE RAIN

SOON, DESPOT RULERS PAID GAGAGOOFY TO FUEL THEIR WAR MACHINES. BUT HE STOLE THEIR FUNDS...BUILT HIS OWN SUPER ARMY...

...AND CONQUERED THE GLOBE, REMAKING IT IN HIS OWN IMAGE! BLEEP! BRRRT!
North Gagamerica
Gagasia
Goofrica
South Gagamerica
Goofstralia

MY DUTY WAS TO STOP THE BUBBLE-BRAINS AND CAPTURE GAGAGOOFY IN 2010...SO THERE MIGHT NEVER BE A PURPLE RAIN...
ZP

...AND I MIGHT SAVE EARTH FROM AN AWFUL FATE...BUT ALL MY EFFORT WAS WASTED.
BUT...
BUT...

WE WANT TO HELP YA, UMA! BUT YOUR OMNI-GADGET DOESN'T EXACTLY HAVE ITS FACTS STRAIGHT!
HUH?

FIRSTLY...PURPLE RAIN PUNCH ISN'T A FUEL; IT'S JUST A WEIRD-TASTING SODA!
SOME MIGHT SAY WEIRD; SOME MIGHT SAY EGG-PLANTY-LICIOUS!

SECOND, THE BUBBLEBRAINS COULDN'T BE *EVIL* IF THEY *TRIED!*
THEY *ARE SO!* AND THE *GRIM GAGA-GOOFY--*

UMA, I'VE KNOWN *GOOFY* HERE FOR YEARS! HE'D NEVER *DREAM* OF OWNING EARTH... HE WOULDN'T EVEN TAKE IT AS A GIFT!
PAT PAT
?!

THAT'S GREAT...BUT *HE'S* NOT THE TYRANT I'M LOOKING FOR.
?

BEHOLD THE VILE VISAGE ON THIS *MONUMENT* TO OUR CRUEL DICTATOR... *THE GRIM GAGAG--*
WAAOH! THAT AIN'T NO GOOF!

THAT'S *PEG-LEG PETE!*
GREETINGS FROM SCENIC MOUSETON
2049

WHUT COULD IT MEAN?
THAT'S WHAT I'D LIKE TO KNOW--

HAR! IT'S SIMPLE, MOUSE! THAT GROSS SODA HAS AN INTERESTIN' BYPRODUCT: IT'S ALSO A SUPER FUEL!

NOW HANDS UP, AND DO WHAT I SAY... OR EAT SLEEPIN' DARTS! AN' WHO KNOWS WHEN YOU'LL WAKE UP-- GET ME?
GASP! THAT'S HIM! THAT'S GAGAGOOFY!

HAND OVER THE PURPLE RAIN SO'S I CAN GET RICH!
GAWRSH, NO CAN DO! THUH BOTTLE'S BUSTED...
SNAP

BUT HERE'S TH' INGREDIENTS-- PENTY O' ASPARTAME!
AND THE RECIPE?

DON'T TELL ME IT'S "UNDER YOUR HAT"--
BUT IT IS! SEE?

HAW! IT'S LIKE STEALIN' A CANDY STORE FROM A BABY! NOW *MOVE!*

WHY DO YOU WANT US UP ON THE *TABLE?* SO WE CAN FINALLY SEE EYE-TO-EYE?
I GOT ME A FUN IDEA TO KEEP YOU FROM MEDDLIN', RAT...

FIRST, WE POUR SOME FRESH WATER...
VOOSH

THEN WE ADD A LITTLE *HIGH VOLTAGE,* AND...
TWANG
RIP!

...PRESTO! A TRULY SHOCKING CREATION! HAR, HAR!
GULP!
BZT
FZT
TZT

NOW, OFF TO THE PATENT OFFICE! I GOT ME A DATE WITH HISTORY!
NAB!

GAWRSH! WE'LL GET FRIED LIKE SHRIMP IF WE TOUCH THUH WATER...A DEADLY, DELICIOUS FATE!
WELL...
FZT
BZT
FZT

...MAYBE WE'RE NOT DONE YET! WE COULD CUT POWER TO THE WIRES...IF WE COULD REACH THAT SPLITTER...
LEAVE IT TO ME!

THIS IS JUST LIKE THE NO-MAN'S LEAP IN AGENT TRAINING--
--HUP--

--FARTHER THAN IT LOOKS--!

TLAK
--WHEW! NO PROBLEM, MOSTLY!
WOW! GREAT WORK, UMA!

I--THANKS! I'M NOT USED TO POSITIVE REINFORCEMENT...
WELL, I SURE TRUST YOU NOW. HERE...TAKE THIS BACK!

CAN'T SAY I KNOW HOW THE THING WORKS, HONESTLY...
SIMPLE! JUST SPEAK WHEN YOU FIRE IT, AND THE TARGET WILL BELIEVE HE IS THE LAST WORD YOU SAY!

BUT WE'RE RUNNING OUT OF TIME! WE HAVE TO FIND THE GRIM GAGAGOOFY, DESTROYER OF--
--OF WORLDS, I KNOW...BUT HIS REAL NAME IS PEG-LEG PETE!

HMM...I WONDER WHY HE CHANGED HIS NAME? HE DOES SEEM TO BE COVERING HIS PEG-LEG RATHER WELL...
113
VOOOMM

PATENT OFFICE
BIG LINE OUTSIDE! PETE HASN'T EVEN MADE IT IN YET!

BAH! THOSE DO-GOODERS DON'T LOOK FRIED AT ALL!
SKREEEE

WHATEVER! FINDIN' OTHER WAYS INTO A PLACE IS MY SPECIALTY!

LET'S SURROUND HIM! GOOD THING WE'RE IN THE LADDER DISTRICT!

HOLD IT, PETE! THERE'S NOWHERE TO HIDE!
WHO'S HIDIN'?
SOMETIMES--IN THE MIDST OF CHAOS--ONE TINY, SEEMINGLY MEANINGLESS ACT CAN TRANSFORM THE FUTURE FOREVER! AN ACT AS SMALL AS THE BLINK OF AN EYE...

OUTTA THE WAY, BEANPOLE!

POK
...THE SWING OF A SATCHEL...

...A CRY OF SHOCK...
STOP RIGHT THERE, VILLAIN! YOU ARE--
ZATT
!
G-G-GOOFY!

I'VE GOT HIM! IS PETE HYPNOTIZED?
I DON'T KNOW! MAYBE? THIS THING TAKES SO LONG TO RELOAD...
TUF
TUF
?
...
?!

NICE TRY, SISTER! I DON'T KNOW WHAT YOU PLANNED...

BUT YOU GOTTA SHOOT BETTER THAN THAT TO HIT OL' GAGAGOOFY! HAR, HAR!
!

BUT...WHY WOULD--
BECAUSE THE LAST WORD I SAID WAS STUTTERING GOOFY'S NAME! THAT MEANS...IT WAS MY FAULT!

IT WAS ALWAYS MY FAULT! ONLY I COULD HAVE CREATED THE MONSTER!
HUH?

THINK ABOUT IT! IF I HADN'T COME TO 2010, LOOKING FOR THE BUBBLEBRAINS AND HYPNOTIZING THEM--
EGGS AN' CHICKENS! THEN I WOULDN'T HAVE VISITED PETE--

AND PETE WOULDN'T KNOW PURPLE RAIN'S SECRET...OR BE "GAGAGOOFY" NOW!
?!
EXACTLY! IT WAS MY FAULT!

I DOOMED MY OWN PEOPLE! I AM THE GRIM UMA-- DESTROYER OF FUTURES!

HOWDY, BOYS! I WANT ME A *PATENT* FOR A BRILLIANT *THING* I JUST INVENTED!
SUCH *MANNERS!* ...YOUR *NAME,* PLEASE?

GAGAGOOFY! YOU'LL BE HEARIN' IT A LOT MORE SOON...

"PURPLE RAIN; ENERGY SOURCE FOR MACHINES! APPLICATION MADE IN PERSON..."
SIGH! EARTH'S FATE IS SEALED!
MAYBE... MAYBE NOT...!

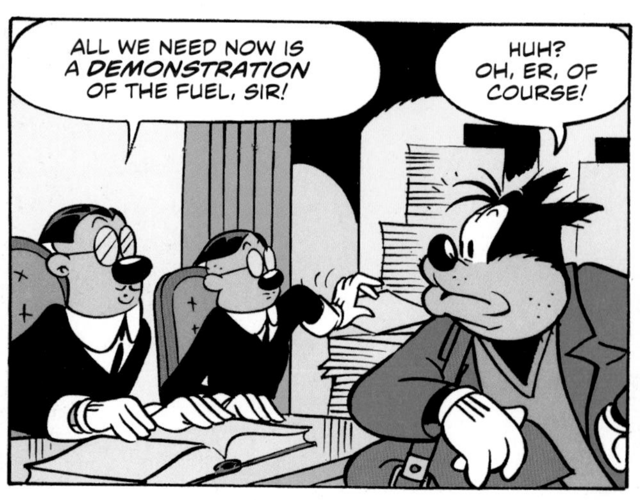
ALL WE NEED NOW IS A *DEMONSTRATION* OF THE FUEL, SIR!
HUH? OH, ER, OF COURSE!

HEH! I GOT ME A BUNCH OF *INGREDIENTS...*

AN' LOOK! MY NOSY ASSISTANTS ARE HERE TA HELP ME!
?
?
?

C'MON IN, PUNKS! YOU WANNA SHARE A PIECE OF HISTORY OR NOT?

WE'LL STOP YOU--
NO YOU WON'T! AN YOU'LL KEEP IT QUIET, TOO...

OR I'LL MAKE YA SLEEP UNTIL YA SEE TWENTY-FORTY-WHENEVER FIRST-HAND!
ULP

NOW WATCH CLOSELY, PENCIL-NECKS... AS I ORDER MY ASSISTANTS TO MAKE MY DREAMS COME TRUE!
PROCEED, I SUPPOSE...

AND SO...
"MIX IN THE POTASH...HOLD SPOON AT 70-DEGREE ANGLE...MUST NOT SING THE BLUES AT ANY POINT..."
...THIS IS GOOFY EVEN FOR YOU, GOOFY...

"...THEN SHAKE IT UP, GIVE 'ER A HOOT AND A HOLLER, AND YOU'RE DONE!"
SHAKIN'? THAT'S MY SPECIALTY!

THAT CAN'T BE ALL! WHAT ABOUT THE SUGAR?
THERE'S NO SUGAR IN THE RECIPE!
GAWRSH, I JUST ADDED THAT ON A HUNCH BEFORE!

BUT WITHOUT SUGAR, IT CAN'T WORK AS A FUEL! IT'S COMMON KNOWLEDGE IN 2049--
HOWLIN' CATS! SO THAT'S NOT REALLY PURPLE RAIN-- YET!

BUT KEEP IT DOWN! PETE WON'T KNOW IT IF YOU DON'T TELL HIM!
?!?
SHAKE
SHAK

LOOKS LIKE YOU CAN *STILL* SAVE THE FUTURE, UMA...JUST NOT THE WAY YOU THOUGHT!

AWRIGHT, MUGS! THIS'LL WORK IN CARS...TANKS...*EVIL ROBOTS...*
WELL, THEN...

...PROVE IT IN OUR *FUEL-TESTING ENGINE,* SIR!
TLIK

KA-CHUNK
HAR, HAR! AWRIGHT, LOSERS! THIS IS WHERE I MAKE HISTORY...

...AN' HISTORY MAKES ME A LEGEND!
GLU
GLU
GLU

FFRRRRRR...
BOP
BOP
HEH...HEH...

BOP
BO-BOP
BIP
BOP
HUH?!

YOU CALL THIS FUEL? WE SMELL A FOOL!
IT'S JUST...UH... WARMIN' UP?
BOP
BAP
BOP
B'-BOP

BLUB!
GO WITH THE FLOW, GANG!

WELL, MR. GAGAGOOFY! UNDER THE CIRCUMSTANCES, CONSIDER YOUR PATENT...

!!
...REFUSED! GOOD DAY TO YOU!
YEAH! THE FUTURE IS SAVED!!
BOOT!

NOW WE'LL USE THUH RECIPE TO HELP MANKIND! SCROOGE MCDUCK OWNS SO MANY GAS AN' COAL COMPANIES, HE'S SURE TA BE INTERESTED IN BUYIN' IT! HYUK!
WHAT'S THAT GADGET YOU JUST USED ON PETE, UMA?
MY DE-HYPNOTIZER! GOOD THING I REMEMBERED TO PACK IT!

AND SO...
DOOFUS B. DAWG, YOU ARE NOT A KANGAROO!
TTAZ
?

DOGUEBERRY... NOT A TRAIN!
TTAZ

AND...
MOOFUS-- OOPS! HOW DOES HE DO THAT??
VOOOM!

GOTCHA!
DURN! JUST WHEN I'D FINALLY LEARNED TA LAND!
TTAZ

THERE!
ALL BACK TO NORMAL...SO TO SPEAK!
TTAZ

FINALLY...
THANKS AGAIN, MICKEY AND GOOFY. I'LL TELL ALL THE HYPERWEB ABOUT YOUR BRAVERY!
I JUST HOPE WE HELPED MAKE THE FUTURE A LITTLE BETTER, UMA!

I'M SURE YOU DID! GOODBYE!
GOODBYE!
FZ
BZ
TZ

POP
GAWRSH! SHE DROPPED HER POSTCARD!
?

WOW! LOOK, GOOFY-- WE DID HELP!
GREETINGS FROM SCENIC MOUSETON
2049
HYUK! THUH FUTURE'S SO BRIGHT, YUH GOTTA WEAR SHADES!
THE END

2049
DIEGO
TAPIE
2010
Sabrina A.

GOOFY in
TOMB OF GOOFULA
Mickey Harker's Journal. May 5. Goofyvania. At last I have arrived at Castle Goofula, Home of Count Goofula. Although the Count appears to be a good fellow, I must wonder if I made the right decision coming here.
WELCOME TO MUH HOUSE! ENTER FREELY AND OF YORE OWN WILL.
KJG-011-1
WELL, ACTUALLY, NOT SO FREELY. HYUK.
E-TICKET RIDES AND FOOD ARE EXTRA.
Castle Goofula
ENTRY FEE
ADULTS 25¢
CHILDREN OF THE NIGHT FRE
SORRY!
NO ADMITTANCE IF YOU ARE NOT AS TALL AS THIS SIGN.
I, Mickey Harker, being of unsound mind, enter Castle Goofula knowing it's scary and dark and probably evil and that I may never leave it again so don't bother looking for me. signed,
Mickey Mouse, RIP
AN' AH DIDN'T MEAN TUH SAY ENTER **OF** YORE OWN WILL. I MEANT **WITH** YOUR OWN WILL. HYUK!

LISTEN, DO YUH HEAR IT? THUH CHILDREN OF THUH NIGHT!
AWOOOOO
AWOOOO! BWAHHH
MOMMY!
PRETTY NIFTY PLACE, HUH? GOT IT REAL CHEAP.
FROM A LITTLE OLD MUMMY WHO HARDLY EVER USED IT.
TOMB OF GOOFULA
BELFRY
LITTLE BATS ROOM

THESE ARE MUH MOMMY AN' DADDY.
EVERYONE SAYS AH'M A CHIP OFF THUH OLD BAT. HYUK.
MAMA
PAPA

I WAS ASKED TO INTERVIEW YOU FOR THE MOUSETON GAZETTE. THEY SAID YOU--
SHUCKS, WE KIN TALK LATER. D'YUH WANT SOMETHIN TUH DRINK?

WON'T YOU JOIN ME, COUNT GOOFULA?
DRINK? AH NEVER DRINK...SODA! HYUK.
MILK, CHOCOLATE, ORANGE JUICE, SHAKES, YUP. JUST NOT SODA.

THEY SAY THAT YOU'RE A VAMPIRE?
YUP. AH REALLY AM! YUH WANNA SEE ME TURN INTUH A BAT?
SURE.
TA DA!
WHY DID I KNOW THAT WAS COMING?
WHAT'S IT LIKE BEING A VAMPIRE?
I'D IMAGINE IT MUST BE GREAT BEING ABLE TO FLY AND TURN INTO A BAT.
SHUCKS, AH DON'T KNOW 'BOUT THAT...
BUT IT SHURE MAKES SHAVIN' REAL HARD. HYUK!
YUH KNOW, VAMPIRES GOT OTHER POWERS, TOO. THEY SAY WE KIN CONTROL ALL SORTSA ANIMALS.
LIKE DOGS AND RATS, AND WOLVES, AND BIRDS. HECK, I'LL SHOW YUH.
TWEET
WATCH ME CONTROL THEM ALL. HYUK!
ARF! ARF! MOO TWEET! MEOW
GROWLLL!
URF!
3

WHAT DO VAMPIRES EAT, COUNT GOOFULA?
GAWRSH. THAT'S JUST IT, MICKEY. AH DON'T LIKE WHUT THE OTHERS EAT. 'T'SO MESSY. HYUK!
SO AH TAKES A LITTLE BIT A THIS. AN' A LITTLE BIT A' THAT. AN' MIX IT ALL TOGETHER.
SUGAR
POP CORN
THERE! WANT A BITE?
ULP!
THAT'S YOUR COFFIN? BUT IT'S FULL OF MUD!
HYUK! YUP! AH GOT IT DIRT CHEAP!
VAMPIRES CAN'T GO OUT DURING THE DAY, SO AH SLEEP HERE WHILE THE SUN IS OUT AN' GO TO WORK UNDER THE FULL MOON.
YOU WORK? WHAT DO YOU DO?
I'LL SHOW YUH. C'MON.
WELL, Y'KNOW, VAMPIRES USED TO TERRORIZE THUH VILLAGERS AN' SUCK OUT ALL THEIR BLOOD.
BUT TIMES HAVE CHANGED. I GOT MYSELF A REAL JOB.
VELCOME TO COUNT GOOFULA'S MONSTER MOVIE MATINEE. TONIGHT VE HAVE A FANG-FILLED FEST OF FEARSOME FLICKS.
STARTING WITH "THE MUMMY GETS UNWRAPPED!" PRETTY SCARY, EH? HYUK!
ch 13
End

WALT DISNEY'S
GOOFY in
TIDY FRIDAY
TIDY FRIDAY! A VERY GOOD IDEA, GOOFY! I'M GLAD TO HELP YOU KEEP YOUR HOUSE IN ORDER! ALL I ASK IN RETURN IS A RIDE TO AND FROM!
YOU'RE A PAL, CLARABELLE! I COULDN'T DO IT BY MUHSELF 'CAUSE I CAN'T STEER GOOD ENOUGH!
W DD 60-04

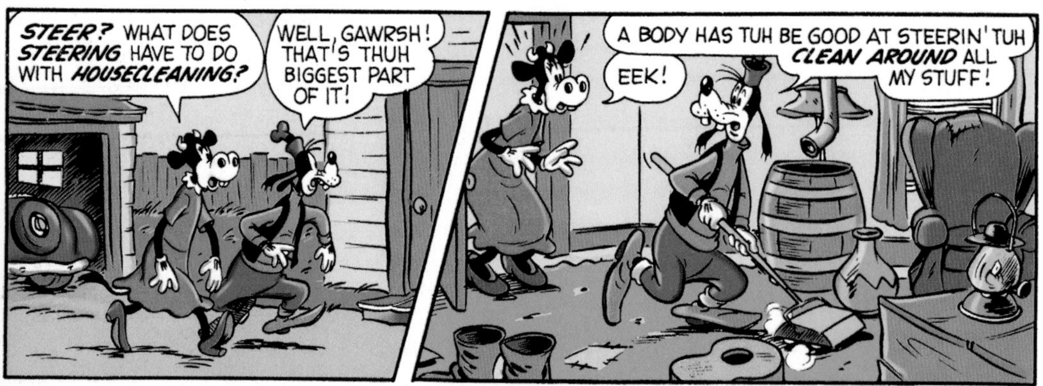
STEER? WHAT DOES STEERING HAVE TO DO WITH HOUSECLEANING?
WELL, GAWRSH! THAT'S THUH BIGGEST PART OF IT!
A BODY HAS TUH BE GOOD AT STEERIN' TUH CLEAN AROUND ALL MY STUFF!
EEK!

BUT I'M FOREVER SIDESWIPING AN' STICKING MUH FOOT IN THINGS!
(TSK! TSK!) THIS PLACE SURE NEEDS A WOMAN'S HAND!

FIRST OF ALL, EVERYTHING HAS TO BE PICKED UP OFF THE FLOOR BEFORE I CAN START CLEANING!
BUT THAT'LL LEAVE MORE ROOM TUH CLEAN!

BELIEVE ME, GOOFY!..THIS IS THE PROPER WAY TO HOUSECLEAN!

UGH! I...I NEVER SAW SUCH HEAVY GALOSHES!

OH, I NAILED THEM DOWN THERE SO I'D ALWAYS BE ABLE TUH FIND 'EM REAL QUICK WHEN IT STARTED TUH RAIN!
AND WHY WOULD YOU NEED THEM REAL QUICK?

LEAKY ROOF!
WELL, YOU CAN PRY THEM UP LATER! I'LL GET ALL THE OTHER THINGS!

HEY! WHAT'RE YUH DOIN', CLARABELLE?
WHY, I'M THROWING SOME OF THIS WORTHLESS JUNK IN THE TRASH CAN!
YAY!

GAWRSH! THAT'S NOT WORTHLESS JUNK... IT'S WORTHLESS KEEPSAKES AN' SOUVENIRS!

(WHEW!) JUST IN TIME!
NOTHING AGAIN TODAY, JOE!
YAY!
TRASH
TRASH
COLLECT

I COULDN'T STAND TUH PART WITH A SINGLE FRAGMENT OF THIS GOOD OL' STUFF!
ALL RIGHT! BUT THEN YOU'D BETTER STORE IT SOMEPLACE OUT OF MY WAY!
YAY!

SHORE! YOU JUST PASS IT TUH ME, CLARABELLE, AND I'LL STOW IT ALL AWAY!
START STOWING AWAY, THEN!
FEB. 1, 1932
DAILY NEWS
YAY!
DANGER

AND KEERFUL! SOME OF MUH THINGS ARE FRAGILE!

AND SEVERAL HOURS LATER...
AT LAST! NOW I CAN START CLEANING!
GAWRSH! I HARDLY RECKY-NIZE THUH PLACE!

SEE HOW EASY HOUSECLEANING IS NOW?
YUK! NOT MUCH OF A STEERIN' PROBLEM! I'LL PROBABLY BE ABLE TUH DO IT MUHSELF COME NEXT FRIDAY!

I CAN REACH THE WINDOWS, TOO, NOW THAT THINGS AREN'T PILED IN FRONT OF THEM!
I'LL HAVE TUH GET SUNGLASSES! NOT USED TO SO MUCH LIGHT!

WELL, ALL'S SPIC AND SPAN! YOU CAN DRIVE ME HOME NOW, GOOFY!
OKEY-DOKEY, CLARABELLE!

OOPS! I MADE A BOO-BOO! ER...WOULD YUH MIND HITCHHIKIN' HOME, CLARABELLE?
HITCHHIKING?!

I SHOULD SAY NOT! WE MADE A DEAL, AND YOUR PART OF IT IS TO DRIVE ME TO AND FROM!
OKAY! OKAY! BUT YOU'LL HAVE TUH WAIT A FEW MINUTES...

I GUESS I JUST WASN'T THINKIN' WHEN I STOWED ALL MY STUFF IN THUH GARAGE! NOW I'LL HAVE TUH EXCAVATE FER MUH CAR!
EEK! I THOUGHT YOU WERE PUTTING ALL THAT IN THE ATTIC!
YAY!

GAWRSH, NO! THUH ATTIC'S ALREADY SAGGIN' QUITE A BIT WITH ALL OF MUH CHILDHOOD TOYS!
CREAK!

BUT YOU JUST GO INDOORS AN' RELAX BY THUH TV WHILE I DIG OUT THUH OLD AUTYMOBILE!
(SIGH!) ALL RIGHT, BUT PLEASE HURRY!

AND LATER...
OKAY, CLARABELLE! I CAN DRIVE YUH HOME NOW... AND THANKS A WHOLE BUNCH!
IT MAKES ME FEEL GOOD, TOO, GOOFY... TO SEE YOUR HOUSE TIDY!

OH... NOT THAT SO MUCH, CLARABELLE! I WAS THANKIN' YOU FOR INSISTING ON ME DIGGIN' OUT THUH CAR TUH DRIVE YOU HOME!
REALLY? ER... WHERE DID YOU PUT ALL THAT STUFF?

WHY, THERE WAS ONLY ONE PLACE LEFT TUH PUT IT, AN' I'M JUST TICKLED PINKISH ABOUT THUH WHOLE THING!

YUH SEE, FROM NOW ON I WON'T HAVE TUH BOTHER WITH DOIN' ANY GARDENING!
The End

A GOOFY LOOK AT ROMANCE
WALT DISNEY
FLOWERS FER YUH, MUH SWEET PINE CONE?
GIGGLE!
THE ACT OF COURTSHIP IS MILLIONS OF YEARS OLD. IT DATES BACK TO WHEN ONLY AMOEBAS INHABITED OUR WORLD!
YOU THINK THESE TWO ARE PLAYING TAG?
DARLING! TRULY, YOURS IS THE SHINIEST MEMBRANE OF ALL!
OH, PHILIP!
NOPE!
IT'S THE SUBTLE DANCE OF COURTSHIP!
...WELL...MORE ADVANCED FORMS OF LIFE!
AND, AS YOU KNOW, AMOEBAS EVENTUALLY EVOLVED INTO...
HYUK!
GAWRSH, THAT FELLER'S ALL GOOGLY-EYED!
HE MUST BE IN LOVE!
COURTSHIP DEVELOPED A LONG TIME AGO, WHEN MEN REALIZED...
...THE CLUB WASN'T THE ANSWER TO ALL THEIR PROBLEMS!

MEN AND WOMEN BEGAN TO COMMUNICATE!
IN ANCIENT EGYPT, COURTSHIP METHODS WERE INSPIRED BY RITUALS OF MUMMIFI-CATION...
I'M NOT SURE I WANT TO BE TIED DOWN!
ROMANS FLASHED THEIR NAUTICAL ABILI-TIES...
RENDER UNTO CAESAR A SUNDAY RIDE, M'DEAR!
WILL YUH TAKE ME SHOPPIN', TOO?
IN THE MIDDLE AGES, MEN WENT FOR HEROIC.
YESTERDAY I BATTLED THREE DRAGONS WHO THREATENED MUH HAYSTACKS!
BUT THE RENAISSANCE EXPLORED COURTSHIP AS BOTH ART AND SCIENCE...
COURTIN' FER DUMMIES

AND THAT'S HOW THE PRACTICE OF *STRATEGIC COURTING* BECAME ACCEPTED...
THUH PROXIMITY OF THUH SUBJECT AFFECTS THUH OVERALL KINETIC FORCE...
$Z(j\omega) = \frac{-L\omega^2 + j\omega R + 1/C}{j\omega}$
$S_1, S_2 = \frac{-R \pm \sqrt{R^2 - 4L/C}}{2L}$
...AND EVENTUALLY BECAME A PROPER TRADE, SEEN BY SOME AS A *PROFESSIONAL VENTURE!*
HYUK!
Diploma
OF ALL THE PROFESSIONALS, THE MOST WELL-KNOWN WAS *CASANOVA*...
...WAIT. THAT'S NOT CASANOVA. THAT'S HIS COUSIN, *OLDSHACK*...
HEY, TOOTS!
WHO TRIED TO FOLLOW IN THE FOOTSTEPS OF HIS FAMOUS RELATIVE...
BEAT IT!!
...WITHOUT MUCH LUCK!
HYUK!
AH...HERE'S *CASANOVA* HIMSELF! SUCH CHARM...SUCH *STYLE*...
RIP
STORIES ABOUT HIS PHENOMENAL COURTING SKILLS - AND THE WOMEN WHO COULDN'T RESIST HIM - PRECEDED HIM EVERYWHERE!
SAY!

SADLY FOR OLDSHACK, THE REAL SECRET OF CASANOVA'S POPULARITY WAS A MYSTERY!
AAAAHHHH...
WHAT'S THAT FELLER GOT WHUT I AIN'T?
IN THE WILD WEST, COURTSHIP WAS OFTEN A COMPETITION, TO BE SETTLED...PERMANENTLY!
A DUEL FOR MUH FAVOR! THUH HORROR!
BUT...
YEEE-HA!
MEN!
...NOT ALWAYS!

GAWRSH!
OH, THUH HUMAN-ITY!
SPINSTER SHELTER
OPEN UP! OPEN UP!!
BAM
NO WAY!
ULP!
YANK!
AND THERE YOU HAVE IT: THE ULTIMATE CONSEQUENCE OF COURTSHIP!
SOB!
PLIK
THESE DAYS, COURTSHIP MIGHT HAPPEN AT THE MALL, DURING SCHOOL OR ON THE INTERNET... THE POSSIBILITIES ARE ENDLESS!
GAWRSH, HE'S CUTE!
DUNNO...HE SEEMS AS SHARP AS AN AMOEBA!
END!

WALT DISNEY'S
PLUTO
HEY! (SPLUT! SPLUT! ...)WHO ?... WHAT THE ...
PLUTO LOVES A DAY AT THE BEACH! EXCITEMENT! CROWDS! AND IT'S SO EASY TO BURY A NICE BONE IN THE SOFT SAND...
W WDC 177-03

PLUTO! STOP! YOU MUSTN'T SCATTER SAND ALL OVER FOLKS!
THAT DOG DOESN'T EVEN BELONG ON THIS BEACH! CAN'T YOU SEE THE SIGN?

ER...NO!
WELL, IT'S HERE.... IF YOU'D BOTHER TO LOOK FOR IT!
NO DOGS ALLOWED ON BEACH

I GUESS YOU'LL HAVE TO GO OFF DOWN THE SHORE AWAYS, PLUTO, AND TRY TO AMUSE YOURSELF!
AND HE'D BETTER NOT SET FOOT ON THIS BEACH AGAIN!

YOU HEARD HIM, PLUTO! BUT DON'T WORRY.... YOU'LL FIND PLENTY TO DO DOWN THERE AMONG THE ROCKS AND DUNES!
SNIFF!

ALL HE WANTED TO DO WAS BE SOCIABLE! HOW CAN A FELLOW BE SOCIABLE ALL BY HIMSELF?
PTOOF!
!

WELL, ANYWAY, NOBODY CAN STOP HIM FROM BURYING HIS BONE NOW!

NOW TO TUCK IT AWAY... HUH?
IT'S GONE!

HMMM... AND ONLY THAT SNEAKY-LOOKING CHARACTER NEAR THE SCENE OF THE CRIME!
Z-Z-Z-Z-Z
?

HUMPH! HE'S JUST TRYING TO LOOK INNOCENT, DECIDES PLUTO! HIS POCKET'S PRACTICALLY BULGING WITH THE EVIDENCE!
G-R-R-R-!
?

AND PLUTO'S GOING TO GET IT!

CLACK!
OW! WHO SLAMMED THE TRAP DOOR?

HE'S PUTTING UP A FIGHT! NOW PLUTO'S SURE HE'S CAUGHT HIM WITH THE GOODS!
G-R-R-R-!
GRUFF!
WOOF!

AH! GOT IT!

HEH! WELL, ANYWAY, HE'S GOTTA ADMIT THERE WAS SOMETHING FISHY ABOUT HIM!

EVERYBODY'S ENTITLED TO ONE MISTAKE... ...BUT WITH PLUTO, IT'S ONE A MINUTE!
SNAP!
EOW!

AND ALL HE WANTED WAS A NICE SOCIABLE AFTERNOON!
O-O-W-W-W-W!

ALL HE ASKED FOR WAS A FEW BEACH PRIVILEGES AND HIS BONE! AND NOW HE HASN'T GOT EITHER!
SNIFF! SNIFF!

HUH? DO PLUTO'S EYES DECEIVE HIM OR IS THAT HIS BONE JUST OUT FOR A WALK!?
?

A TURTLE! SO THAT'S IT!

IF THIS OL' TURTLE LIKES TO CARRY THINGS SO MUCH... LET'S SEE HIM DO SOME REAL CARRYING!

WELL, WHAT DO Y' KNOW.... HE CAN! AND THAT'S WHEN PLUTO STARTS GETTING IDEAS!

ALL OF A SUDDEN HIS PROBLEM IS SOLVED!
HEH! HEH!
HEE! HEE!
HOO! HOO!
HEE! HEE!

SHORTLY...
SAY! I TOLD YOU THAT DOG WASN'T SUPPOSED TO SET FOOT ON THIS BEACH!

I KNOW! I TOLD HIM, TOO... AND HE MUST'VE UNDERSTOOD ME 'CAUSE... HEH... YOU CAN SEE FOR YOURSELF...

...HE SURE ISN'T SETTING A FOOT ON IT!
THE END

PLUTO

EXCLUSIVE INTERVIEW WITH CASTY!

International superstar creator Casty (a.k.a. Andrea Castellan) has produced a much-loved variety of work since beginning to write Mickey Mouse stories in 2002. His stories feel modern yet timeless, sending Mickey Mouse and his friends on thrilling adventures built upon their vast history yet always adding new dimensions. Two volumes of his work now appear on American bookshelves: the epics MICKEY MOUSE AND THE WORLD TO COME, and MICKEY MOUSE ON QUANDOMAI ISLAND. This volume marks the third American collection of the writer/artist's work, and there's sure to be more to come!

Casty was kind enough to take some time out of his busy schedule to answer some questions from us and from his fans...

***KABOOM!:* You've featured a wide variety of Mickey's "rogue's gallery" in your stories - from Pete to the Phantom Blot to the Rhyming Man, and even insects from the far future! Who is your favorite Mickey villain to use, and why?**

Casty: It's hard to say which is my favorite, because every one of them has some peculiarity that I love. But I have to say I have really enjoyed "resurrecting" the Rhyming Man, who is in my opinion the meanest villain Mickey has ever met. He's so cruel, and so strong, that I was almost afraid he could really get out of my hands and do harm to Mickey! He's a really bad rogue...and that's why I hope we won't see him for a long time!

I love when villains act "seriously," because this allows you to create a story with tension and suspense. Nowadays, too often you see stories where Pete (and/or the Blot) look like they are almost "clumsy idiots," or stories where they are almost Mickey's friends, going bowling or on holidays together. Mickey needs real enemies to be a believable hero!

Because of the "softening" of these classical enemies, some years ago I created a new recurring villain for Mickey: his name's "il Magnifico Doppioscherzo" ("the Magnificent Doublejoke") and he's sort of like Batman's Joker, with megalomaniac purposes and an army of yellow, smiling robot-toys. He has really hated Mickey ever since they were schoolmates! Doppioscherzo has had a very good reception in Italy and Europe, and I have written five stories featuring him so far. I hope one day you can read them in the USA. I'd like to know what readers think about him!

How did you get the idea for the awesome space hotel Olympus in "Mickey Mouse and the Orbiting Nightmare"? And now that there's a huge weapon orbiting earth...will readers discover what became of it after the end of the story?

Mickey Villain "The Magnificent Doublejoke"

I needed an original location for a classically-structured suspense story à la Agatha Christie, with a group of characters trapped somewhere and dealing with a mysterious threat. These kinds of stories are usually set in an isolated place. I had already used an isolated manor in one of my first stories, "Topolino e lo sguardo del Basilisco" ("Mickey Mouse and the Eyes of the Basilisk"), so this time I was looking for something really original. The idea popped out when I read about a billionaire who paid a lot of money to be hosted on the space shuttle.

What became of the Olympus after the story? Well, I think it was probably dismantled...

For "Menace from the Future," you created a whole extended family for Goofy, each with their own unique look and behavior. What was your inspiration for these characters, and do you have further plans for them?

Some of Goofy's distant relatives in "Mickey Mouse and the Great Goofoonga"

In Italy, Goofy has traditionally had a huge number of relatives, uncles, nephews and cousins, and I think this came to us from US stories such as Floyd Gottfredson's "Goofy Doctor X". So it was natural, for me, to create a set of "Bubblebrain" Goofs, coming from different countries. I don't have any plans to use them again, but who knows...

I've also used Goofy-like characters in several other stories, such as "Topolino e le macchine ribelli" ("Mickey Mouse and the Rise of the Machines"), set in a town where all the inhabitants have an extraordinary similarity with Goofy. And there's even a lost island in "Topolino e il grande Pippunga" ("Mickey Mouse and the Great Goofoonga") which is crowded with little pigmy-esque Goofy characters. I've recently written a story where Goofy has a relative who's supposed to be "the last man on the moon"...so, you see, Goofy's family tree is long and continually updated!

Uma's look and design feel like a great modern/futuristic update of the classic Disney model. What did you consider most important when you designed her?

From left to right: Uma, Eurasia Tost, Estrella Marina

Uma is just the last one of a trio of "cute, brave and adventurous girls" I have created to motivate new adventures.

In the mid-2000s, Mickey's adventures were becoming very predictable. The canvas was always the same: Chief O'Hara asks Mickey for help, Mickey arrives and the guilty party is Pete and/or the Phantom Blot. So, I thought it would be good to create some new characters, new partners and/or enemies to bring some fresh air to Mouseton.

The first one was Eurasia Tost, an intrepid archaeologist. Then came Estrella Marina, a cute and brave oceanographer. They both, with their naïveté and youth, helped return a bit of that "sense of wonder" to Mickey's 80-year-old world.

And last came Uma, a chronautic agent from 2049. All these characters have been carefully designed to be Disney-like: their shapes are based on the classical Mickey structure and their suits are easily recognizable and simple to draw. Uma was the most difficult to design, because in the beginning she had to appear to be a bad guy, so I needed to give her a "dark look."

Will we see Uma again - and her world in the year 2049?

Probably so! The story is called "Mickey Mouse and the Tide of Centuries." It's already written, but it still needs to be approved by my editors. It's a long and very complicated story, with time paradoxes and a lot of action. This time, Uma, Mickey and friends have to face "the end of the world as we know it" and a very dangerous villain…it won't be as easy as it has been with Pete!

Can you give us some hints on the next epic you have in the works?

Besides the new story with Uma, I have several plots in my drawer. I tend to alternate between longer, epic stories and lighter ones, so that I can decide what to produce next according to the time I have at my disposal, or according to my editors' requests. The next one I'm planning is a "supernatural" thriller, where Mickey has to fight against a mysterious kidnapper made of dead leaves(!), who hides in the forest near Mouseton. Another story I'd like to do this year is about Mickey, Goofy and Eurasia following the footsteps of Colonel Percy Fawcett and looking for the lost city of Zeta.

Many of your stories have included environmental messages. For readers who share your concern about the state of our planet, what advice or instructions could you give them on how to help make sure the desolate future in MICKEY MOUSE ON QUANDOMAI ISLAND never comes true?

Thank you for this question! It allows me to talk about a matter that's really important to me. You know, I often read internet comic forums and reviews…and I see that every time I speak about ecology, someone pops up and says: "Oh, not again! It's the millionth time he's brought this up!"

Well, when I write these kinds of stories, I think of the children: for them, this is not "the millionth time" they hear this story. That's why I think it's good to do so, using a funny and entertaining way of talking to them about respect for our planet, for the animals…and for mankind. One thing should be clear: I never start a new story planning to teach anything. If you just want to tell the kids how bad it is to dirty the world, they quickly get bored. I just try to tell an interesting story, basing events on what's happening in the world…then it's up to them to learn, if they want to.

I also often speak about the value of things such as friendship, and honesty, and selflessness…and I'm glad I have Mickey as a testimonial for this. Mickey has the power to talk directly to your heart: in "Mickey Mouse and the Orbiting Nightmare," just look how quickly Cassandra Dot converts when Mickey shows his disfavor to her methods!

I hope one day you'll have the chance to read "Mickey Mouse and the World of Tutor," a story of mine published to celebrate the 40th Earth Day. I think this is the story that better shows my idea of "interesting story that even teaches something!"

SOME INSIDE JOKES
FROM CASTY

DID ANYONE NOTICED THE GUILTY WAS... ON THE COVER?

HERE HE IS! THE PHANTOM BLOT! JUST TURN THE COVER UPSIDE DOWN!

WHILE MICKEY IS INVESTIGATING, WE NOTICE A "FAMILIAR PROFILE" HERE....

...AND WE SEE HIM AGAIN HERE...

"A-HA!"
-SOME SAID AT THAT POINT.
"I KNEW THE GUILTY WAS PETE! AS USUAL!"

"A-HA!" - I SAY - IT'S NOT PETE... HE'S ACTUALLY AN INNOCENT COOK!

LOOK!

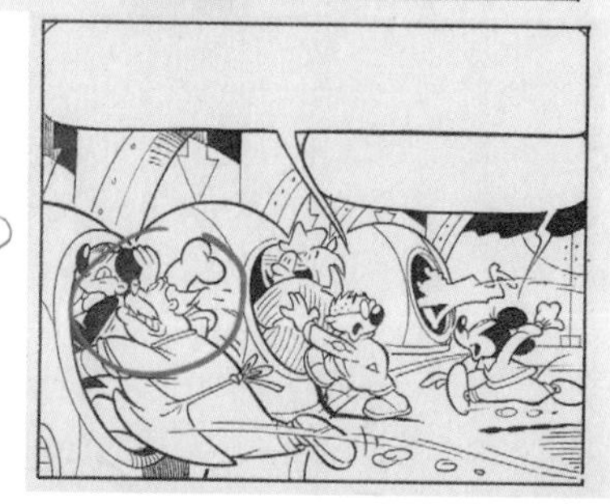

Presenting here an alternate ending to "Mickey Mouse and the Orbiting Nightmare!" This ending ultimately wasn't used in the final story…which is good news for Mickey!

CASTY TAKES YOU BEHIND THE SCENES OF

IN THE VERY FIRST VERSION OF THE STORY (NEVER DRAWN) UMA WAS A ROBOT (U.M.A. = UNITA' MOBILE ANTROPOMORFA = = ANTROPOMORPHIC MOBILE UNIT). A GOOD ROBOT, SENT BY HUMANS TO STOP GOOFY. IN THE FINAL SCENE SHE REVEALS THE TRUTH...

ALL THE READERS WOULD HAVE CRIED!

MICKEY MOUSE AND THE MENACE FROM THE FUTURE!

The Evolution of a Page: from Rough to Finished

See how a page from "Mickey Mouse and the Menace from the Future" took shape, from rough layouts to final, polished artwork!

STORYBOARD PHASE

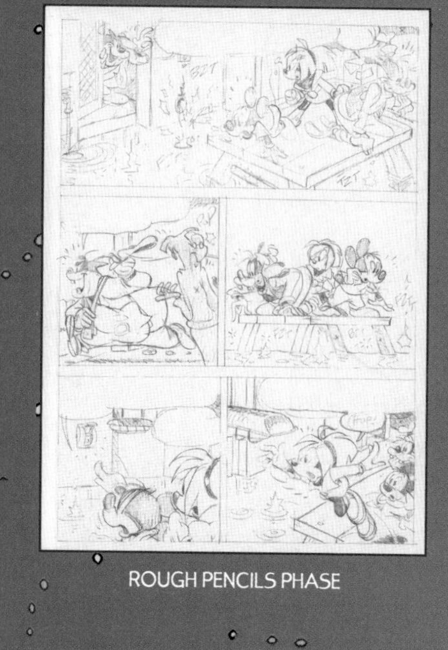

ROUGH PENCILS PHASE

FINISHED PENCIL PHASE

INKS PHASE

COLORS PHASE

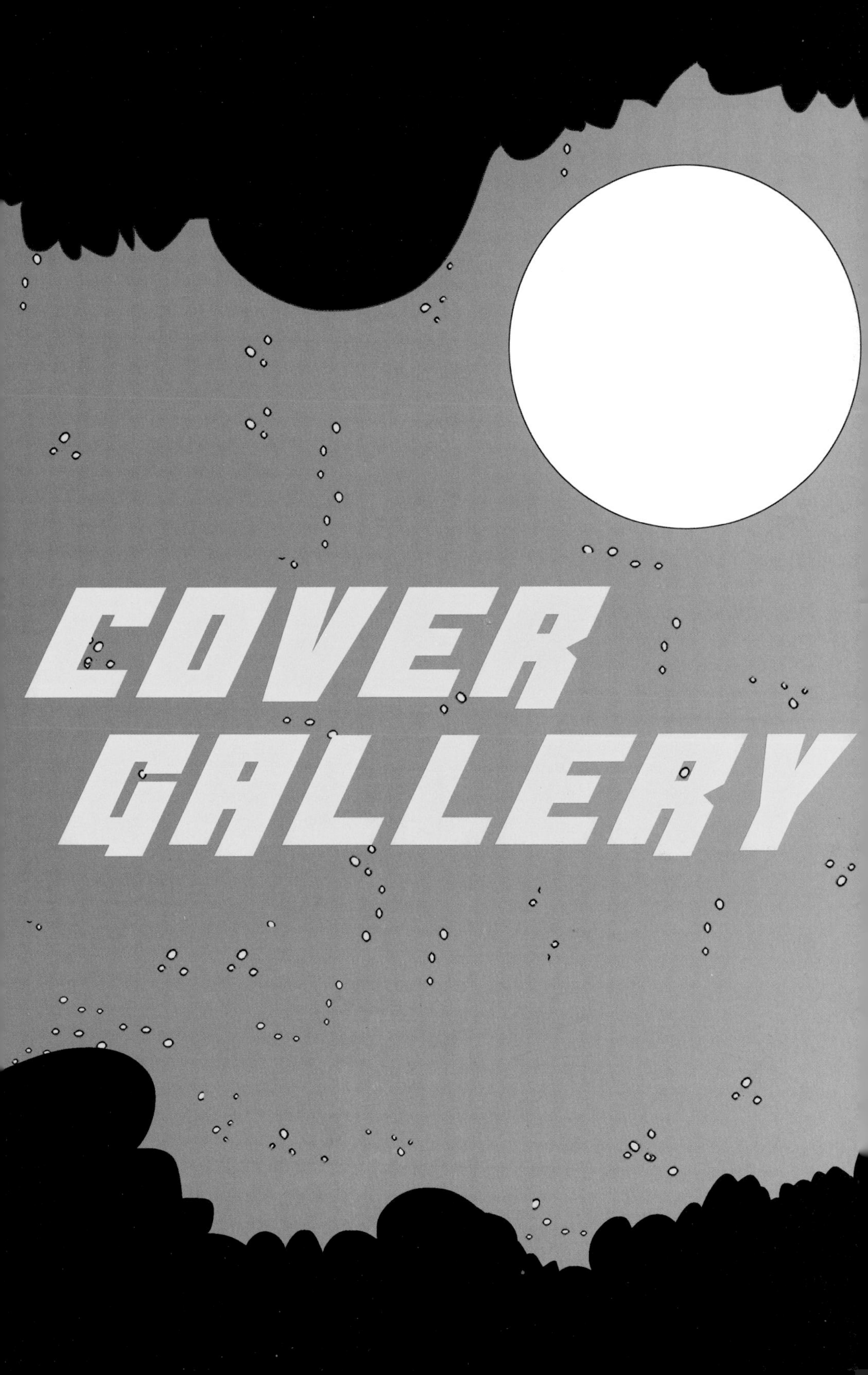
COVER
GALLERY

CASTY

Magic Eye Studios

Colors: Mike Cossin

Casty and Sandro Zemolin

2049
DIEGO
TAPIE
2010
Sabrina A.

CHECK OUT THESE EXCLUSIVE PREVIEWS OF OTHER GREAT TITLES NOW AVAILABLE FROM

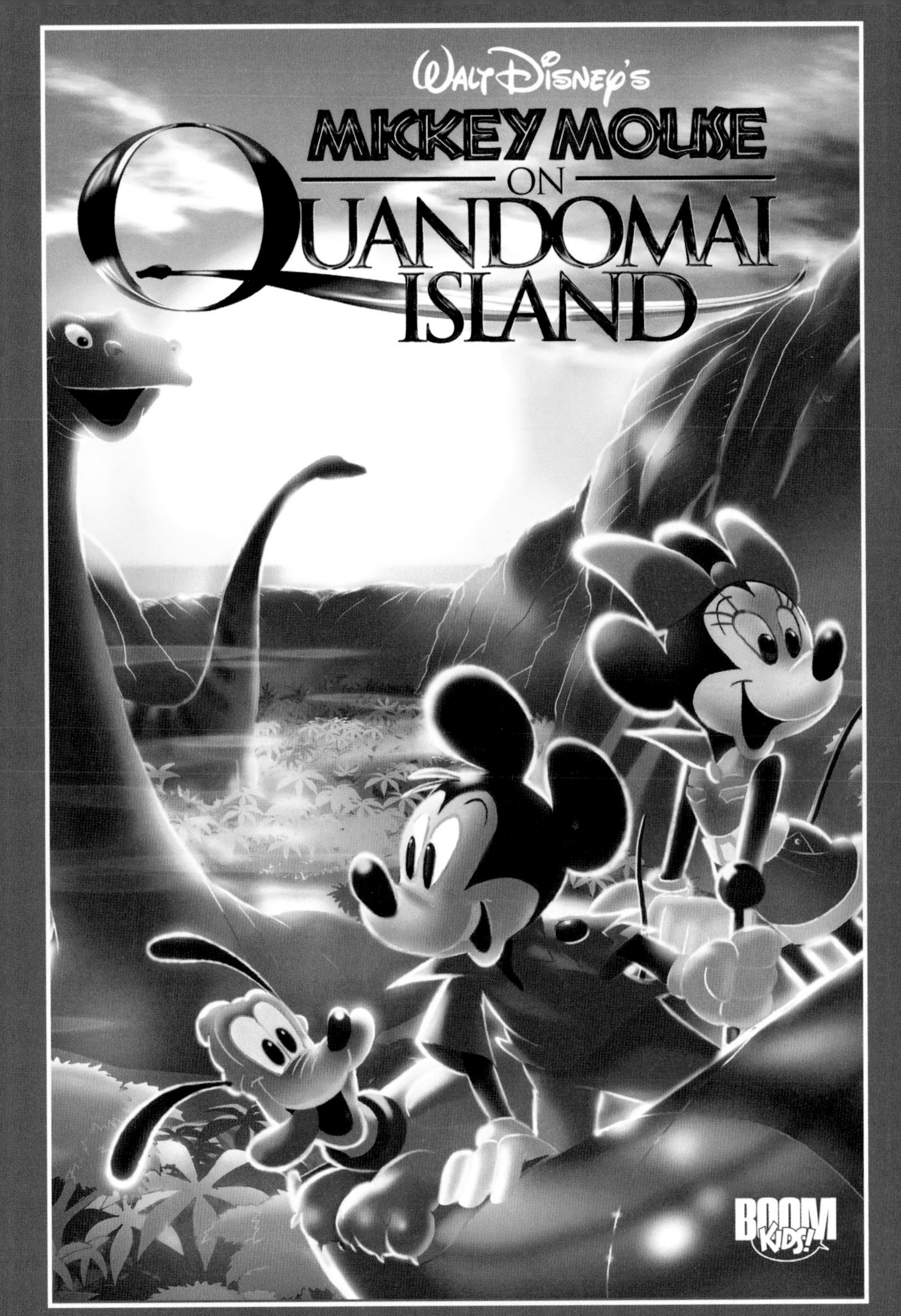
WALT DISNEY'S
MICKEY MOUSE
ON
QUANDOMAI
ISLAND
BOOM KIDS!

"TWICE FIVE MILES OF FERTILE GROUND," INDEED! SHALL WE EXPLORE, MILADY?
GLADLY, DUKE!
HMM...

HOLD THE PHONE! YOU HEAR THAT?
SOUNDS LIKE BRANCHES BREAKING...
?
CR-ACK...

IT'S LIKE THE-- THE FOREST'S ALIVE!
AW NO! IT WANTS REVENGE FER THAT TIME I MOWED MUH LAWN!
CRACK
CROCK

OVER THERE, TOO! WHATEVER'S HAPPENING, IT'S GETTING CLOSER!
CROCK...

GOOD GRAVY! I CAN'T BE SEEIN' THIS!
SO THAT'S WHAT THOSE SCIENTISTS WERE STUDYING!
GASP!

DINOSAURS!
A WHOLE DOGGONED VALLEY OF 'EM!

AIN'T ALL OF THEM GIANT LIZARDS SUPPOSED TO BE EXTINCT?
LOOKS LIKE THEY GOT BETTER!

MUCH AS I HATE TO BREAK UP THE OGLING...WE SHOULD GET BACK TO SHELTER BEFORE THAT RAINSTORM COMES BACK!
RRUMBLEE...

AND SO THEY DO...
JUST THINK, TRUDY! WE COULD MAKE A FORTUNE TURNIN' THIS JOINT INTO A TOURIST TRAP!
HAH! AND WHO SAID THIS ISLAND BELONGS TO YOU, GOOD SIR?

MAYBE YOU AIN'T HEARD OF THE INFAMOUS PEG-LEG PETE, DUKEY...
KEEP YOUR TOY PLUGGED. THERE'S A GOOD LAD.

NOW, IF YOU WANT TO MAKE SOME REAL MONEY OFF THIS ISLAND, YOU'RE GOING TO NEED MY INTELLIGENCE AND EXPERIENCE. I SAY WE...
PSSST PSSST PSSST
HUH!
OH...

DUKE, YA BRILLIANT DUKE--THAT'S BRILLIANT!
OF COURSE IT IS, AND I'LL THANK YOU TO TELL ME SO AGAIN AT DINNER. NOW, DO WE HAVE AN UNDERSTANDING?

WE SURE DO, YA... HOLY--!!!
SOMETHING AMISS? YOU LOOK LIKE YOU'VE SEEN A GHOST!
FLASH

NOT YOU!
NOT HAPPY TO SEE THE BEAGLE BOYS?
716-167
617-716
761-1

BECAUSE WE WAS HAPPY TO SEE YOU! AND FOLLOW, OF COURSE!
716-167

MY DIAMOND! LAUNCHPAD, YOU HAVE TO STOP THEM!
HOW, MR. MCDEE? IT AIN'T LIKE I SAW THIS COMING!
THAT WAS THE PLAN! SCROOGE LEADS, BEAGLES WAIT!
716-167
617-716

THEN WHEN YOU FIND US SOME TREASURE, WE NAB IT!
716-167

UUH, IS THIS SUPPOSED TO...
CLICK!

AAAGHH!

SUDDENLY, WAY UP ATOP THE TUMULUS...
SHIKT

LOOK OUT! I'LL SAVE YOU!
NOT AGAIN!

BOOM!

CHICKA-BOOM!

SO THAT'S HOW THEY GOT THEIR NAME! CAN'T SAY I'M SHOCKED!
I WOULDN'T BE SO SURE!

YOW! SOMEONE JUST TURNED THE POWER BACK ON!
CHICKA-BOOM!

AH, AN OLD LESSON, LAUNCHPAD! THE LIGHTS COME ON AND THE PESTS SCATTER!

AND NOW TO TAKE WHAT IS RIGHTFULLY--

EEP!
YOINK!

IDIOT! I DEMAND YOU PUT ME DOWN!
SORRY, MR. MCDEE! THAT ELECTRICITY'S STILL CHARG-GIN'...
LOOK! THERE'S AN OUTLET!
MY DIAMOND!

...RIGHT FOR US! STORMS ARE A LOT HARDER TO RUN FROM THAN FLY THROUGH!
BUT MY DIAMOND!

YIPES! WHERE'S SMOKEY THE BEAR WHEN YOU REALLY NEED HIM?

MY! DIAMOND!
LOOK, MR. MCDEE! I RESPECT WHAT'CHA SAY, PRIORITIES AND ALL. REALLY! BUT FORGET TH' DIAMOND--

...AND BEAT FEET!

Disney's
DARKWING
DUCK

SO MEGAVOLT, YOU THOUGHT YOUR PLAN TO HOLD STARDUCKS FOR RANSOM WOULD SUCCEED.
YOU THOUGHT YOU FINALLY FOUND THE ONE THING THAT KEEPS ST. CANARD AWAKE AND ALIVE.
BUT YOU DIDN'T COUNT ON ONE PERSON. ONE PERSON WHOSE DETERMINATION AND ALERTNESS WOULD STILL BE AT MAXIMUM POWER EVEN AFTER RUNNING THE MOUSETON MARATHON!

BECAUSE I AM THE TERROR THAT FLAPS IN THE NIGHT! I AM THE AWKWARD GOODBYE THAT LASTS FOR FAR TOO LONG!
I AM
DARKWING DUCK

AND SO WE COMMEMORATE THE ONE-YEAR ANNIVERSARY OF "THE STARDUCKS CAPER," THE LAST KNOWN ADVENTURE OF ST. CANARD'S MASKED AVENGER, DARKWING DUCK!
SODA
SNAC

BEFORE THE DAYS OF THE QUACKWERKS CORPORATION, ST. CANARD DEPENDED ON UNLICENSED VIGILANTES WITH, AT BEST, QUESTIONABLE TASTES IN FASHION.
QUACKWERKS

WHAT TASTE IN FASHION?

A FAR CRY FROM THE SAFE STREETS WE HAVE TODAY THANKS TO QUACKWERKS'S CRIMEBOTS!
FOR THE QUACKWERKS SATELLITE NETWORK, I'M CHIP DIPSON! DIP DOPSON WILL BE BACK TOMORROW.

4 SALE
ATTENTION QUACKWERKS EMPLOYEE GROUP 421! THERE IS A MEETING ON FLOOR 142! THE MEETING STARTS AT 2:41! ATTENDANCE IS MANDATORY!